THE

GIRL

HE LEFT

BEHIND

THE

GIRL

HE LEFT

BEHIND

A NOVEL

BEATRICE MacNEIL

HARPERAVENUE

The Girl He Left Behind
Copyright © 2020 by Beatrice MacNeil.
All rights reserved.

Published by Harper Avenue, an imprint of HarperCollins Publishers Ltd

First edition

HarperCollins books may be purchased for educational, business,
or sales promotional use through our Special Markets Department.

HarperCollins Publishers Ltd
Bay Adelaide Centre, East Tower
22 Adelaide Street West, 41st Floor
Toronto, Ontario, Canada
M5H 4E3

www.harpercollins.ca

Library and Archives Canada Cataloguing in Publication

Title: The girl he left behind : a novel / Beatrice MacNeil.
Names: MacNeil, Beatrice, 1945- author.
Identifiers: Canadiana (print) 20200182579 | Canadiana (ebook) 20200182587 |
ISBN 9781443460651 (softcover) | ISBN 9781443460668 (ebook)
Subjects: LCGFT: Novels.
Classification: LCC PS8575.N43 G57 2020 | DDC C813/.54—dc23

Printed and bound in the United States of America
LSC/H 10 9 8 7 6 5 4 3 2 1

Dedicated to Dawn and Sheldon Currie
and for their beloved Rachel, ever present

Prologue

WILLOW ALEXANDER IS A CELTIC BEAUTY. HER large green eyes are epic in thought as she paces around her kitchen like a jungle cat, watching and listening from window to window for any sound or movement beyond her door. She runs her fingers through her wild reddish mane. Her naked body trembles, a moment hot, a moment cold, a moment unrehearsed as she waits on this thirteenth of May 1985, her birthday, for the police to come and arrest her.

It was Willow who found their bodies. In the upstairs bedroom, there was a leftover smile on Kathleen's face as she lay in her bed. Dr. Millhouse was in his office, with his eyes half-open, as though he were watching death approaching down the stairs. The autopsy reports are still pending. The Mounties are investigating. The last time Willow saw the Millhouses, she and Kathleen were having tea in their favourite china cups. Willow had gone to visit with Kathleen the night before they died. Dr. Millhouse had taken his tea in his downstairs office.

"Mysterious and strange," people rumoured, "that they died together like that."

The only thing visible beside their bodies were the beautiful bone china cups. Still half-full of tea.

‡ ‡ ‡

BEFORE THE POLICE come to question her, Willow decides she must rid the parlour of its photos. The gold-, silver- and wooden-framed smiles of her dead relatives were on display on a fading doily on the side table beside a window. She has decided to burn some of them and will pack others in a trunk and have her neighbour store them for safekeeping while she is in jail.

Nobody has tapped on her door all day, and she has ignored the ringing phone. Willow drops the photos of her maternal grandfather's relatives into the flames of the kitchen stove. The photos curl like worms poked with a stick. They are the relatives she's never met or ever cared to meet. Willow is soon covered in soot as she continues organizing things before the police arrive. She can't leave anything behind when she is taken away. She does not want any intruders destroying the dignity of Murdoch Alexander's home.

At eight o'clock that evening, a cool fog surrounds the Alexander house like a net. Willow listens as a heavy rain shower begins to fall, creating little silver brooks that float down the windowpane.

Willow realizes she forgot to give Sorrow, her pet crow, his special treat. Willow pulls the switch on the small lamp in the parlour as she leans her back up against the wall. She waits, just waits, in the dim light like a drifter in an empty church.

The next morning, Willow wakens to the sound of banging at her porch door. She grips the edge of a chair to help herself up off the floor and quickly pulls on an old track suit and her rubber boots. She doesn't remember falling asleep. It has stopped raining, and the sun is now blazing in through the window. When she opens the door, two Mounted Police officers are standing on the step.

"Are you Willow Alexander?" asks the woman officer. An older male officer stands at her side. They exchange glances. Willow recognizes them as they introduce themselves. They were patients of Dr. Millhouse. And she knows they recognize her as well. The introductions are only a formality, she suspects; in their line of work, they have to introduce themselves even to someone they know.

"I'm sure you are aware of why we are here," the male officer says.

"Awareness can be a contemptuous vice, officer. I've been watching for you," Willow responds.

"We would like to ask you a few questions down at the station, Miss Alexander. We know you knew Dr. Millhouse and his wife better than most people in Glenmor," the male officer continues formally.

"You can wash up before we go," adds the woman officer, as though she were speaking to a lost child.

Willow's voice is direct. "I don't need to wash up. My answers will be the same whether I'm dirty or clean."

Again, the officers exchange glances. The woman officer returns to the cruiser, makes a call, and then brings a package of wet wipes from the cruiser and hands them to Willow.

"Is there anything you'd like to do before we leave, Miss Alexander?"

"Yes, sir, I would like to feed my pet crow. I forgot to give him his treat yesterday."

Willow trained Sorrow, a year or so ago, to call out her name. *Willooo*, it caws, whenever she brings him a special treat.

Willow calls out to the crow but gets no response. She drops the treat on the gatepost, knowing the bird will find it later. The woman officer helps Willow gently into the back seat of the police car. Willow opens the back window and looks out just as the crow lands on the fence post a few feet from the cruiser.

"Listen, listen!" she cries as the male officer gets behind the wheel and prepares to leave. "Sorrow heard my voice."

Sorrow caws loudly, *Willoooo!*

The car pulls out of the driveway, the engine purring softly as they drive down the lane to the police station.

==

CHAPTER ONE

Ghosts

Christy's Mountain, the grande dame of Glenmor in the northern highlands of Cape Breton, holds the sun close to her breast at dawn, slowly weaning slices of light down over the village to embrace the freshly fertile seeds that were planted in early spring.

The mountain's beauty is seductive and playful, haunting and inviting, swaying in the deepest greens and golds, with a pitch-black hue in her craggy seams. After dark, young people will gather like fireflies carrying lanterns to listen for the haunting, ragged voice of the man whose young bride vanished years ago into thin air before his eyes, never to be seen again. Legend has it that he stayed on the mountain to sing to her in their mother tongue, with his powerful Gaelic, pleading voice, hoping she might return to his side.

As a child, Willow had rolled her eyes when her mother

told her of the singing ghost. Now, at forty years of age, she allows a sprinkle of amusement to smear her disbelief in such tales. Secretly, she catches a thrill when the lanterns stop moving after dark, their flames held up evenly until the screeching begins. She hears the screams and sees a parade of lanterns rush by her house on the run. Willow applauds the screech owl. He has scared them once again after all these years.

A busy breeze combs the uneven shades of grass covering the Alexanders' property. The "sun patches," the wide-open, deeper-green fields of Glenmor, stretch for miles. Paler greens whisper near the back porches and along the verandahs' borders.

The Bent River is close by. Full of winter's gifts as it flows. Dead black branches twisted like wire, snapping. The wind offers up to the river the bleached carcass of a small wild animal. A child's blue mitten coils around its rib cage by loose strands of wool. The river is respectful of its cargo. It runs smoothly and its voice is as thrilling as the whippoorwill.

From the village barbershop, a slant of grey smoke thins out from the stovepipe as it rises to mingle with a low cloud. A small sign on the door reads OPEN DAWN TO DUSK. Inside, the tea is always piping hot. The old yellow dog, beside the stove, is bilingual. His owner, the barber, who lives in the back of the shop, is a wise little man who knows and keeps every secret that flows from the lips of his customers. Sometimes a customer or two will stay so long, it is said he will need another haircut before he leaves.

Beside the barber shop, the Country Corner Store opens its creaking door at 7 a.m. Sharp. The owner, a cranky, stout woman in her sixties with eyes as cold as a winter stone, checks her doorbell, which acts as her guard dog when she has to go out back to slice bologna and other slabs of meat. She stands in the doorway of the back room, meat cleaver in hand, to check out who has entered.

"Oh, it's just you," the shop owner whines. "Just you" is never named. She turns the doorbell off when she's behind the counter, her hawk eyes alert, all-knowing. She knows where every item is located. She counts every peppermint in the jar at the end of the day. One can't run a business on blind faith.

On Saturday afternoons, the kids gather around in front of the barbershop as Felix the fiddler rosins his bow. At his feet is a small wooden box beside the fiddle case. He will raise his hand to stop anyone from dropping a coin in before he plays. He wears a long, dark overcoat down past his knees. A fedora is perched to the side of his head. He is young and he is old. In disguise and fully exposed. He can speak, but never a word leaves his tongue. He saves his words for his widowed mother, who cares for him, a mile beyond the Bent River. In his face are the colours of a pastel painting—gentle blue eyes, a pale, creamy complexion with strokes from the sun's brush on his cheeks. His mouth is the fading hue of a dying rose. His hair, sprinkled with silver, hangs down past his collar.

Felix scans the crowd with his soft eyes. He knows what music lives in the feet of the dancers. He begins with a jig and the kids form a circle. Dust clouds the air. Dogs scatter for a quiet place. The bell from the Country Corner Store howls in protest.

The music grows closer to their feet, thundering up the ground, as Felix rattles the bow into a strathspey and reel with ease. And when the music stops, the older men move closer to the musician, standing as still as choir boys. The bow trembles and weeps into a Scottish lament. Nobody moves. No birds fly by. Children stop talking. The old bell from the Country Corner Store is silent. The barber stands on his step, ignoring the tears rolling down his face. Felix's body moves in rhythm as if the music is breaking out through his skin. His eyes are closed, and when they open, they roll and close again in a quiet, quivering ecstasy. And then the music stops, and the silent musical genius of Glenmor prepares to leave. He closes the wooden box full of coins, packs the fiddle away in its case and moves in long strides towards the Bent River Road, oblivious to the applause that follows him like a clap of thunder.

On Monday mornings, circles of schoolchildren gather along the sides of the country roads, along with a dog or two, as a yellow school bus wheezes around a turn and halts to a stop. They file in one by one as the dogs wag their tails and wait until the bus is out of sight before they return home. The children ride along as the day brightens, past clotheslines of freshly washed sheets, drifting like square clouds in the greening fields. Gentle and innocent laughter sneaks out an open window and is carried off to the sea. The younger children hug the driver before they leave. He calls them by name as he helps the smaller children down the steps.

Glenmor's fishermen are already on the sea, muted specks of colour seen from the shore when the sun rises. There are generations of families on the bending waves, burly eighteen-year-olds working side by side with their fathers and grandfathers. The eyes of the elderly, misty with knowledge, watching carefully.

"Keep an eye on the sea and an ear to the wind," they warn from the stern of the boat. "What watches you must always be watched. Nature has her own set of rules!"

The old priest, in the parish church for daily Mass, raises a circular white host in mid-air before it is broken. Between his knotted fingers and thumbs, he divides it carefully and swallows it delicately. He too is respectful of his cargo. He adds a silent prayer for the safety of the fishermen dividing the waters of the Atlantic.

‡ ‡ ‡

WILLOW ALEXANDER AWAKES before dawn. She has been dreaming in colour about the dead, but she is with them in this dream, a child in a green plaid dress, matching ribbons in her hair. Nobody appears to notice her watching them go by. The others are all grown women, walking in single file towards a pasture with the word *Paradise* scrolled on a wooden plank set against a tree. In the lead, her beautiful mother, pale as spring frost, smiling as the others follow her. Behind her is Kathleen, Willow's dear friend, and wife of Dr. Millhouse, whom she worked for recently at the clinic. Kathleen had not walked on her own for some time before her passing. In the dream, she moves like a dancer, the tip of one golden shoe cupped in her hand in mid-air, the other touching down on soft sand along the path.

Kathleen was a brilliant woman and a psychologist, gone now after what seems like years, yet it has only been weeks. Willow's mother would have called the Millhouse deaths a mixed blessing, since Kathleen and Dr. Millhouse left this world together. It was an ending Willow's mother might have wished for herself when her husband, Murdoch, died at age fifty. Her husband's death left her with the sacraments of bereavement, the distance that the heart has to cover in order to bleed out its denial, its anger, its sorrow and finally its acceptance, her passport for moving on. Willow believes her mother never really knew what distance she had covered after her husband passed away. Rhona Alexander died less than four years later, shortly after revealing the intimate details of their wedding night to Willow. The memory makes Willow chuckle despite it all.

In Willow's dream, a young woman moves slowly from a shadow behind the others, her black hair in French braids, her smile a dangerous red. Willow attempts to speak to her, but the woman doesn't seem to notice her. And suddenly, as the procession reaches the pasture, they all disappear.

Willow believes the unknown woman is the one she and her lover, Graham Currie, fashioned a fictional story around for years. Willow had always imagined her with hair as black as midnight. Her name is Mary Ann MacIver, a teacher and spinster, as she is referred to when her name is spoken, who passed away in 1867. Beside her in the Journey's End Cemetery lies John Duncan MacSween, a bachelor, who died a week after Mary Ann. Graham and Willow spun tales like cotton candy about the spinster and the bachelor. Mary Ann refused his offer of marriage and left his heart as empty as a dry well. He became a recluse, seldom seen, except at sunset, that seam between dawn and dusk when the heart is most vulnerable, when he'd venture out into his field to watch the orange sunset before returning to silence behind his locked door. Willow is a frequent visitor to their graves in the old section of the Journey's End Cemetery.

It is 3 a.m., hours before the dawn will bloom, and Willow's room is surrounded by the dead. She is not frightened by the dream. The dead looked very content. On the go, even. Mary Ann, vibrant, with her full red mouth visible. Where were they going with her lovely mother in the lead? What lay ahead in the pasture? The lead was something Rhona Alexander had rarely taken in her life. Willows smiles at the image of Kathleen, the dancer, her small hand cupped around a golden shoe. Willow can't remember her role in the dream, or if she ever made it to Paradise. There were no men in the dream. Perhaps they were already there, waiting. Maybe there is no need for love beyond the point of no return. Or was the dream a reflection of her life at the moment? Alone. Pale-lipped. And she has not danced in years.

"Dead end," she mutters to herself as she pulls the quilt over her head.

Under the blanket, Willow's dream lingers. How would Kathleen, her dear friend, have analyzed this dream? A child dressed in plaid. Willow hates plaid. She wishes she had Kathleen's insight on this one.

CHAPTER TWO

==

Silk Kites at Dawn

ROM THE KITCHEN WINDOW, WILLOW WATCHES A
pair of cardinals—a rare sight in Glenmor—mating
on her wild rose bush. She is sure that the female
is deliberately keeping her beak closed as long as she can
while her masked suitor offers up seeds, beak to beak, in
the artful aggression of hormonal mating. Perhaps it is
Mother Nature herself who sets the discord. The female's
olive plumage with its reddish-tinged tips is no match for
the male's rich crimson plumage. Sweet whistles marinate
the soft wind as the male's wings burst in mid-air. The morning sun sets a golden yoke upon them as they fly towards
the tall trees and disappear.

Willow cannot imagine how the so-called experts, whoever they are, can tell that cardinals mate with the same
partner for life. The idea of grown men and woman recording the sex lives of birds in the trees makes no sense to her.

Useless information annoys her like an open pin on bare flesh. For some reason she regards it as another form of male domination.

She pulls down her blind as the bold sun flares into her kitchen. The room is spotless, its perfection disturbed only by her light footsteps moving towards the flames in the kitchen stove. She has let the fire settle into a blue haze, while a shiny steel kettle gargles up a head of steam. A bowl of oatmeal, drowned in cream, sits marooned at the back of the stove. In silence, a pot of tea brews. The green tea-pot cover lifts slightly, takes a short breath, then sinks back down. In a moment of fading memories, Willow gives the calendar a quick eye. The red circle around the thirteenth of May surprises her. Why had she bothered to lasso her birthday, now two weeks past already? At forty, she tries to ignore any intrusion of celebratory reminders.

She believes that most woman begin to lie about their age at this point. New lines mingle with the old but are forgiven. She has kept her hair a darker reddish of late. Strange that both her parents' hair remained immune to the fading effects of time until they passed away.

Willow pours a cup of tea and follows her own silence through the open parlour door. In this room the private beauties of innocence surround her. Fading lace doilies hang like chipped fingernails from the antique tables. An old blue horsehair couch with three cushions is backed up, as if by force, against the long wall. A matching chair hovers in a corner. Beside it stands the wooden ashtray in the guise of a butler that her father made before she was born. In his black-and-white tuxedo, he is always on duty, his eyes alert. A hawk-shaped nose embellishes his superior stance. His name is Henry, and in the hands of this warrior of smoke and ashes is an empty tin ashtray painted with wildflowers by her mother sometime before her death.

Willow sits and places her cup on the mahogany table beside her chair. A collection of dead family members stares back at her. She is happy now that she did not destroy all the photos and instead stored them in a trunk. They are back on display now. She feels the comfort of having rescued them. She looks at the photo of Jacob Alexander and his soft, petite bride Bella, Willow's paternal grandparents, newly united. Draped in satin, with a tangled bouquet of roses and ivy in her hands, Bella stares back. A look of terminal bliss on her young face.

Willow's grandparents on her mother's side, Edith and Sid Cropper, are also there, in a wedding picture that was taken in a studio in Boston. Edith was barely seventeen when she left Glenmor and went to Boston to work. A fake palm tree stands near the bride, who is seated in a crooked wicker chair. She is wearing open-toed pumps with fabric bows that match the material in her slim lace dress. The groom, in a pinstripe suit and white shoes, is heavy-set and bald. A judge from Boston. He died six months after the wedding.

There is only one photo of Willow's parents' wedding.

They are standing in a damp field of daises with their arms around each other. There is no way of telling how tightly they held hands behind their backs. They were never physically demonstrative; they were silently in love. The climax of their days, a sudden smile during a meal. The gentle collide of two shoulders as they left the table. Stealing touches of each other while their child watched. Willow remembers her father's patchy voice on his deathbed.

"I love you, my dear Rhona. I always have." Impending death made a public romantic out of the stoic Murdoch Alexander.

There is no wedding photo of Willow. She was to be married to Graham Currie in June of 1970. A wedding that didn't leave the altar and didn't leave photos behind, as far as she knows. There is only Willow's memory of pews filled with stretched, pale faces watching nervously for the tardy groom to appear, sneaking looks at the bride-to-be in the foyer of the church. Waiting. The silent organ. The grand "Wedding March" cold on the sheet. The stoic Willow, her father silent at the end of her arm. He knew. He knew. Her mother, fuelled by anxiety, anticipating a wake instead of a wedding. She was sure the groom was dead. Killed on his way to the church. These things happen.

"At least he'll have a new suit," Rhona whispered, pacing back and forth in the foyer.

People turned towards the front of the church, their whispers spreading like dominoes from pillar to post. They had no reason to stay and no reason to leave. Not one of the groom's family members was present in the front pews to ease the growing gossip. Willow could hear the whispers, people wondering where the Currie family was.

Marjorie, her best friend and maid of honour, in a blue gown, whispered, "It'll be okay, Willow. Just keep your chin up!"

It was her father who suggested that they leave. The old priest, his glasses at the end of his nose, his skin lined like corduroy, strode down the middle aisle of the church, his right hand in mid-air as though he were directing traffic.

"Has anyone heard from the young man?" he inquired. "Where is the Currie family?" His curious glare set upon Willow in a strange yet pitying glance. "Is there a reason for this delay? The young man looked rather peaked at the rehearsal last night?"

Murdoch Alexander spoke quietly to the old priest. Willow didn't listen to their conversation. She removed the train from her gown and flung it on a bench in the foyer. The creamy white of her dress mated with the clouds floating above the open doors as she walked down the steep stairs of the church towards the calling sea.

‡ ‡ ‡

WILLOW TURNS HER attention to the scene above the fireplace in the parlour to clear her head of an approaching

headache. The oil painting of her and her father on her fifth
birthday is always comforting. They're in a clearing a quarter
of a mile from the house. To the east, Christy's Mountain is
shedding its morning dew. A soggy, yellow-eyed sun stares
down the mountain. On this birthday, the thirteenth of
May 1950, the forecast called for a salty breeze and spotless
sky in the village of Glenmor.

That morning, thirty-five years ago, Willow could smell
the smoke that drifted on the air from their wood stove.
Her father was standing close to her, giving her instructions
on how to release her kite. "It has to catch the even breath
of the wind," he said. "This is the secret. It will go nowhere
without a whisper of wind to guide it."

"Are you really sure, Daddy?" she asked.

"As sure as I am that you are five, Willow."

Her mother had designed the kites from leftover scraps
of silk from her sewing basket. Willow's name was embroid-
ered on the full-shaped yellow moon, and six small gold
stars trailed behind. Murdoch attached a wooden handle to
a long silk string to complete the masterpiece. The kite's
extended wings stretched out over a wire and thin strips of
wood. Her father had made a kite for himself to fly along
with Willow's, a fighter-bomber replica from one of his war
books. He had fashioned arrow-shaped points in the middle
of each kite for leverage. Streaks of red, blue and deep vio-
let soared towards the troubled clouds.

Murdoch balanced the handle in his fingers as delicately

as if it were priceless lace. Willow's small hands uncoiled the string of her moon kite in slow motion. She felt a slight pull as the kite took flight. When the west wind shifted, the two kites were almost parallel. And when the sun escaped behind a dark cloud, Willow watched as the kites snarled in mid-air and the tail of stars hit the mountain. Her father pulled her into his arms as the rain fell hard, leaving dimples in their bare flesh. Her mother followed close behind with her head damp and bowed, like a martyr off to the stake. It had been her mother's idea to go out at dawn "to catch the fresh light."

Back at home, Willow and her father drank hot chocolate as her mother's artistic eye circled a reflective take on the morning's events, creating a vision for her painting. The sun, the light, the rain and the dead kites aligned in her mind. She stood a makeshift wooden easel in the middle of the room facing the window, a stretched canvas placed on top. Jars of paint—burnt umber, raw sienna, cobalt, yellow ochre—were placed in a row alongside.

Rhona Alexander was not a particularly good artist. She strolled through the village looking for inspiration and stroked from her brush at what she perceived as fresh tragedies: The steeple of St. John's Church struck by lightning for the third time. The collapse of the Bent River Bridge after a flood. Haunted houses with no windows and doors, the wind, wild with freedom, belting a chorus of raw pleasure in and out of the empty rooms. The Daughters of Salvation

Convent defiled by graffiti once again. Rhona had offered this particular painting to the Daughters, but they politely refused. There was no way they would hang anything that couldn't be blessed on the convent walls, and prayed violently for the graffiti artist to reform. He was exceptionally talented, yet under the wrong brush. The graffiti artist's latest painting, the naked man by Michelangelo, was anatomically correct, they firmly acknowledged. Rhona believed that one day her paintings would hang in some archive and collapse into the historical dust of rural life in Cape Breton.

Young Willow walked slowly to the east window and looked out towards the great mountain. Its stark beauty gave her no hint that any of the small stars or the full moon from the kite could be rescued. She moved slowly past the blank canvas, empty only temporarily, until it was stained into a memory by her mother's furious strokes.

"Do you know where my kite and stars are, Daddy?" Willow asked, her eyes wide.

"They were caught in a wind shift, child."

"Can the wind send them back to me?"

"I don't think so, Willow," her father answered. "The mountain has what's left of them, tangled and torn off in the trees."

"Who has the other part of them?"

"The wind has probably carried them to the Bent River, and the river has dropped them off to the sea."

Through the years, Willow developed a habit of counting stars in the night sky in clusters of six. And now, thirty-
five years later, an allusion to astrological omens still has
the power to stretch her imagination.

Now, standing face to face with her mother's painting
above the fireplace, even after time has altered its freshness,
its morning colours and maternal intentions, Willow finds
new traces of that spring morning in its simple, amateur
strokes. Her father's hands are large and obedient, tattooed
with calluses from his life as a lumberjack. His shoulders
are broad and straight. His bright-red, wavy hair is stranded
over his eyes by the wind. The kite looks like a toy in his
hands. He is wearing a plaid shirt, open at the neck, sleeves
rolled to his elbows. He is handsome in the way muscular
men carry themselves into the hearts of delicate woman.
Willow is dressed in a green short-sleeved blouse under her
dungaree overalls. One of the straps has fallen down the
side of her arm in a tomboy sling. A small-boned child with
strawberry-blond braids laced in ribbons, a bold twist of
exasperation minted on her lip. She is holding the kite up
to show something to her father. He appears attentive, his
large hand on the kite, like on a wound that requires special
care.

Willow is now trying to remember what she asked her
father on that fifth birthday so many years ago. Teacup
in hand, she stretches her feet out in front of the chair
to think. What had she pointed out to him that needed

attention? It comes to her now. Dug up from some child-ish notion that even silk stars had to be aligned, she feared a crooked silk star could never rise. He untied the string and convinced her that they were in perfect alignment. The word *aligned* settles in her ear. Something wiry and dark is remembered too. Her father hadn't shaved that morning. She'd touched his face when he bent down. Her small hands followed a map of coarse stubble; she warmed them against the flame of his breath. Her mother had not captured this image in her painting of father and daughter. Perhaps she didn't know how to mix a colour for such an emotion.

CHAPTER THREE

Murdoch's Destiny

MURDOCH ALEXANDER, WILLOW'S FATHER, grew up near the Bent River Bridge in a family of twelve. He inherited his red locks and long legs from the peninsula of Kintyre in western Scotland, which he believed heightened the Alexander legacy. His father's forebears came to rest squarely on two feet beside the deep waters of northern Cape Breton in the 1800s, the new land's wild winters and sprawling woodlands not all that different from the old country. When time allowed, young Murdoch read on the bank of the Bent River, from mail-order books, the lives of Proust and Voltaire, Galileo and Aristotle.

After Murdoch's father, Jacob, died in his sleep in his mid-forties, Murdoch's long-suffering mother, Bella, prayed amongst the trees and kept a secret conversation going with the saints. Young Murdoch never knew what Bella prayed

for in the woods. His fate was sealed in the burning torch
he now carried as the oldest in the family. He was sixteen
years old when his mother became a widow. He instinct-
ively assumed the throne of fatherhood and his new life as
a lumberjack. He never finished eleventh grade, his dream
of becoming an engineer falling further out of reach with
every tree he dropped. He was grateful that his next two
siblings were strapping boys, already reaching six feet.
They were experienced enough to help with the outside
chores. The girls were already cleaning the house and preparing meals.

Glenmor frosted early in October of 1931. Ghosts
and goblins, including the younger Alexander children
at Murdoch's insistence, trampled a mat of golden leaves
underfoot and wandered from wooden door to wooden
door for treats. Weary housewives, who smelled like sugar,
dropped fudge and taffy apples into their opened pillow-
cases. Their husbands kept a vigil on the outhouses with a
lantern in hand. Every child became daring at Halloween,
their great devious pleasure the coveted image of a victim
emptying his or her bowels in a tipped-over outhouse.

‡ ‡ ‡

"How are you today, Mother?" Murdoch asked in his new
role as man of the house. He was chewing on a piece of
fudge swiped from his youngest sister's loot.

"Full of old sorrow," she replied. "The saints don't hear the prayers I leave between the trees. Are you murdering my prayers with an axe, Murdoch?"

"I'll make you a cup of tea. You must be weary."

"Where are the others?" she asked.

"In school, Mother. They'll be home soon."

"Why aren't you in school today?"

"I stayed home to be with you. To keep you company."

"I don't need company, Murdoch. I need a husband."

He left the kitchen and opened the porch door quietly and stood on the back step. Emotional scenes left a dry crust in his mouth. He could not form a sentence. What advice could he give his mother? He had never watched a man die before. And this was his own father. He had never comforted a grieving woman before, especially someone as fragile as his mother. Death, as it was understood in the mountain, came with its own mercy to the suffering.

The lonely drone of the school bell echoed down the mountain. For a few moments, young Murdoch placed himself back in the seat of knowledge. He inhaled the smell of old books from the shelves at the back of his classroom and traced the initials carved into the wooden desks. He heard the sluggish whistle of the worn, blue-veined map being pulled down over the blackboard. He felt his teacher's trembling hand on his shoulder on his last day of school, a touch that had left a chalk mark on his blue sweater.

"You were my brightest student," said the teacher as she turned to erase the blackboard and wipe a tear from her eye. "The world needs minds like yours, Murdoch Alexander. I wish you well."

But young Murdoch was pragmatic, and he knew these dusty images of his last geometry lesson belonged to the past. At sixteen, he could not disappoint his father.

Two of his mother's older spinster sisters arrived when Murdoch's father died. Their first task was to air out the straw-filled mattress upon which the stains of conception of the Alexander clan lay embedded in a dark groove. They whisked and scrubbed the house from top to bottom. Cookies and biscuits and little cakes bulged out of cupboard doors and tin cans. The children were lined up and inspected for loose seams and head lice. Bella, Murdoch's thirty-five-year-old mother, sat in the corner of the kitchen rubbing her sore knees, her dark eyes collecting the emptiness surrounding her. Her sisters took no notice of her. She had been a smart girl at one time, had agreed to marriage as though it were the Triple Crown, they said, and ended up with a dead horse. By this they meant money was thin. The house was too small. Germs thrived in every corner. Some of the children had carrot-coloured hair. Bella's deceased husband, they claimed, although a hard worker and good-natured, had had an addictive amorous nature that kept his wife forever in the family way, with little time for airing out her straw mattress.

CHAPTER FOUR

Knowledge on a Window Ledge

ON HER FIRST DAY OF SCHOOL IN 1950, WILLOW Alexander watched a crow perched on the outside window ledge near her small desk. It stayed so long without moving, she believed it was wounded.

"I see we have a girl who doesn't pay attention on her first day of school," said the high-pitched voice of the middle-aged schoolteacher. She pointed her ruler at Willow. "Stand up when spoken to, child!"

Willow stood up, stiff as a rod, beside her desk. She kept one eye on the crow, who hadn't moved an inch.

"Willow Alexander," bellowed the exasperated teacher, "you have no doubt been sent to school to learn reading, writing and arithmetic, not to gaze at crows, wild things that I am not overly fond of and never will be."

Willow eyed her teacher like roadkill. Dismantled hair was permed to her head like shredded wheat. Her uneven teeth clacked. A pleated tartan skirt rose shorter in the front. Dusty penny loafers were too tight for her feet. And the pennies were missing. Willow knew she would never like this teacher who didn't like crows. Willow knew crows were very smart, and she could tell that this crow was in pain.

To Willow's left sat pretty Marjorie MacInnis, biting her lip, who would become her best friend despite her nervousness and endless chatter. To her right was handsome Graham Currie, soft-voiced and slightly sweating, a dark curl in the middle of his forehead, who would become her lover. In the back row sat a scowling older girl. She grinned at Willow with her thick reddish hair and fancy clothes. The girl wore a faded tartan skirt and white blouse that was too small for her plump body. When she raised her hand, two of her buttons popped open. Willow was wearing an over-dressed creation of silk and lace like an underaged call girl.

"Miss, I think the poor crow is injured, and I was wondering if I could help him at recess," Willow said firmly.

"There will be no need for that. I will have our janitor get rid of the bird as soon as possible. This is not a crow hospital. It is a place to learn."

Willow crinkled her nose at the teacher. "Is he gonna kill him? I don't believe injured creatures should be destroyed."

The teacher made a quick sign of the cross before mumbling to herself, "It is a school for higher learning. Perhaps some of you would like to rise above a ruffle of feathers."

Willow moved closer to the window to look at the bird. The class fell silent. She was out of line. The class understood that "pay attention" meant you didn't move, even for the red-haired girl in satin and lace. The teacher reached into her pocket for a blue pill before returning to her desk and slumping into her chair.

The crow continued to watch.

"Sit down, Willow, and pay attention to your lesson!" the teacher reminded her again.

The crow disappeared when Willow returned to her seat. At recess, she found the janitor and asked about the bird.

"What happened to the crow that was perched on the window ledge?" she asked him.

"It had a wire wrapped around its foot," he said. "I cut it off and away it flew." The janitor smiled at Willow.

"If he comes back," she said, "put him in a box and I will take him home and my daddy will help him. I don't want you to kill it, mister. I named him Ralph."

The janitor tapped her on the head and went back to work. "I'll keep an eye on the crow." He smiled at her.

Willow requested plaid dresses and pleated skirts as she entered the kitchen after her first day of school. "I want to look like the other girls at school. That's what all the girls wear," she told her mother.

The following day, she and Marjorie shared lunches. Graham Currie walked by drinking from a jam bottle full of a powdered drink mix. Willow had a new pink Thermos that she shared with Marjorie, then gave it to her to keep. The next day Willow came to school with her milk in a jam bottle.

By grade three, eight-year-olds Willow Alexander, Marjorie MacInnis and Graham Currie were one ripple in a small brook, a poem without an ending, a link of innocence, wisdom and defiance. They were not nocturnal yet, as Graham had to be home before darkness fell, except on Halloween, when they travelled together as masked children of the night. One ghost and two scarecrows, carrying flashlights with fresh batteries as they travelled farther along the dark paths of Glenmor at Willow's request.

"The Journey's End Cemetery is just over the hill," Willow half whispered. "My mother said the dead are allowed out around Halloween for a few days. They deserve a break."

"I wanna go home," Marjorie cried.

"You're staying at my house tonight, and there's no school tomorrow," Willow reminded her.

Graham shone his flashlight towards the wrought iron gate of the cemetery. It was wide open. They were on their own. No adult supervision. Everyone felt safe in the mountain village of Glenmor. It was their fortress compared with what happened in places far away where, Willow's mother believed, they had to check their children's treats for nails and razor blades before the kids could eat anything.

"Why are the dead allowed out?" Marjorie's question combined curiosity and fear.

Willow's answer was swift: "To check things out, Marjorie. They lived here too, at one time. They won't bother mortals as long as we pray for them."

"What are mortals?" Marjorie asked.

"Kids like us. Now let's go!"

Graham was a short distance ahead. He was running his flashlight through the slats in the fencing. Willow and Marjorie caught up to him. They watched the dim light settle on slabs of marble and wooden crosses, and the smaller crosses where babies and young children were buried. Some of the crosses were tilting towards the ground. They listened for a while to the sounds of the night and watched as the stars popped out like popcorn over the cemetery, as on any other clear evening in Glenmor.

Willow and Graham were disappointed. They left because they were bored. Marjorie chewed on a piece of fudge as they walked away from the dead, who had not returned on their free pass. They had not risen to check out what held their bones in one place, or why their crosses were on a tilt, what had been chiselled on their stones about them, or if someone whispered their name as they strolled by.

The children were not quite around the turn when a white mist dropped down over the Journey's End Cemetery and someone or something moved slowly along the path.

It was Graham who faintly heard the clanging of the gate being scraped along the ground. But he did not mention it to Willow or Marjorie.

In grade six, Marjorie played the Virgin Mary and Graham was Joseph in the Christmas pageant. Willow played a sheep. She was thrilled as an eleven-year-old not to have to play the part of Mary. Willow was too tall. Mary, she believed, was less than five feet in height and was not a redhead. Willow gathered all the grade six girls in the gym.

"If you vote for Marjorie to play Mary in the Christmas pageant," Willow announced, "you are all five dollars richer." She flashed a fistful of bills from her saving envelope marked *Chore Money*.

The girls rushed forward.

"Not so fast," Willow flared. "Marjorie hasn't made it to the manger yet."

The vote was twelve for Marjorie and one for Willow. Willow smiled when Marjorie confessed that she had voted for her to play the blessed Mother Mary.

During summer vacation in July of 1959, before the trio entered ninth grade, they hiked at daybreak up Christy's Mountain as far as they could go. Willow hung coloured ribbons on the trees to mark their trail. She had packed a lunch for three and brought bottles of water. Marjorie brought gum and a whistle. Graham, the healer, brought bandages and fly lotion. At one point, Marjorie believed she heard a black bear, but the others convinced her it was the wind. They pretended they had conquered part of Everest at the midpoint of their hike and put a stake on a flat peak with their signatures on it. Then they sat on the ground and ate their lunch.

When the three friends arrived back at the bottom of the mountain, a furious Mrs. Currie waited until she was face to face with her son.

"What have I told you about climbing anything with girls?" she wailed. "It's bad for your health. You could have fallen and broke yer neck." She caught her breath. "Did they make you do anything you didn't want to? Show you something you've never seen before?"

"Marjorie showed off a cat scratch, Ma. Willow showed me her new climbing boots. That's all," Graham pleaded. "And I wasn't out of breath once. We never slid once. We had a rope. Willow can do anything with a rope. She was in the lead. She knows the mountain better than anyone around here."

"A girl in the lead always leads to trouble," his mother retorted. "You stay away from her. Now get in the truck. Your father needs your help at home!" She turned on Willow with a warning. "You stay away from my Graham! He'll make a fine doctor one of these days, if he doesn't fall to his death because of your carelessness."

Willow twisted the rope she was carrying into a noose and held it up to show off her skills. "Graham's right, Mrs. Currie. I can do anything with a rope."

Mrs. Currie, pale-faced, moved closer to her old truck. Graham followed her. In a panic, Marjorie ran towards the Alexanders' verandah. Willow's parents were in the city for the day.

"I don't want to have to tell you this again," shouted Mrs. Currie from a distance. "My son will be a doctor one day if he stays away from you!" She jumped behind the wheel of the old truck and sped away in a cloud of dust. Graham's head could barely be seen above the dash.

Marjorie ran over to Willow after Mrs. Currie drove away. "Why is she so mean to you? We didn't do anything wrong to Graham. We didn't kick him or punch him."

"My father told me not to be rude or mean to her," Willow replied. "He said people protect their own in ways you won't understand until you're older. Much older."

"But . . . but Willow . . . you made a noose." Marjorie hesitated before going any further. "Were you going to use it, Willow?"

"Not today. I just wanted to let her know she doesn't scare me, Marjorie. And besides, she doesn't know I will marry Graham Currie, come what may."

Marjorie's eyes widened. "Did you tell Graham yet? How will he know if you don't warn him? His mother will be so mad."

"He'll know when he's older and can understand things. Now let's go make some pancakes!"

‡ ‡ ‡

IN SEPTEMBER, WHEN they returned to school, Graham was not in the same class as Willow and Marjorie. His mother had had him transferred to the other grade nine class. At lunchtime, Willow sought him out. She found him alone at the back of the school with his back to the brick wall.

"What the hell is going on, Graham?" Willow asked. "You don't belong in that class. It's going to slow you down. Most of those poor likeable kids can't read two words."

"I tried to tell her, Willow, but she wouldn't listen." His face was pale, his eyes hazy from lack of sleep.

"Then tell your father. Or speak up for yourself!"

"It's no use. She just tells him to shut his mouth and let her handle things." He reached for Willow's hand. "I miss being with you and Marjorie. I never know what you're going to say or do. You make me laugh. I don't laugh at home."

"Meet me after school in the cemetery," Willow said. "I have something to take care of right now."

"You're not planning to bury anyone, are you?" Graham called out to her.

Willow laughed as she ran towards the front of the school and headed for the principal's office. At five foot seven, Willow Alexander was a galloping beauty.

Graham watched her run off, allowing his eyes to linger on her back, observing the changes in her stride, the ripple of the strong muscles in her legs, the way her red mane caught the wind. His throat felt as though he had swallowed sand. He took several deep breaths, slid his back down the brick wall and sat on the ground. Who was he kidding? His mother had already seen the changes in his attitude towards Willow. She'd caught him staring at her school picture. He felt different now around Willow. Felt an awkward shyness, a coil twisting in his stomach when she looked him in the eye. A boldness at night, as he reached out to her under his hot quilt and placed her hand where his mother could no longer look or touch. Spread his legs to fit her in and carve his name on her skin like a bruise. He knew he loved her. He always would, he whispered to her under the quilt.

Who could he tell? No one. He longed to ask an adult what he should do next, but he couldn't ask her father. They were too young. He knew her father would be kind and understanding with him, but he would ask Graham to wait until he finished his studies. But he didn't want to wait. Graham just wanted an adult's advice on what he should do while he waited. He dropped his head between his knees and wept.

Everyone referred to the school principal as Sir Jim, and he coached the volleyball and basketball teams in the school gym. Willow ignored the secretary when she said Sir Jim was busy and flung open the door to his office. A wooden coat rack fell like a heavy drunk towards the edge of his desk. Sir Jim's hand dropped his sandwich, and he began to wheeze as he reached for his phone.

"I beg your pardon, Willow Alexander," rolled out between Sir Jim's teeth. He was a passive-aggressive, grim-faced man who clung to life on the tailcoats of temporary mercy. He was "from away," although the location of "away" was never revealed. "I would have expected a cordial tap at my door from someone of your upbringing. You are a brilliant young lady with a great future, not a runaway mare."

"And I would have expected you to keep the brilliant Graham Currie where he belongs, Sir Jim," Willow answered, addressing him head-on. "You know he should never have been taken out of his regular class, no matter what his crazy mother has to say."

"I don't see this as a concern of yours, Willow. This is a school matter and really none of your business. I shall not discuss school matters, especially with a belligerent student such as yourself."

"The money my mother gives to this school should really—I mean, *really*—concern you at this moment. Graham Currie should not have been moved to another class. And I am positive my parents would agree with me on this one."

Sir Jim dropped the phone. Willow stood the coat rack back in its place and left. She headed for the cemetery and was leaning against Mary Ann MacIver's headstone when she saw Graham walking down the path towards her. They would be sixteen in the spring, yet his six-foot height and slight build gave him the appearance of someone much older. Willow knew that, one day, Graham Currie would be trained and reliant on a career in medicine. He would stand between life and death as a healer to the people of Glenmor. And by then, his mother would be old or out of the picture altogether, and she, Willow, would be beside him, making him laugh on and off the mountain peak. She was sure of that.

"He has a soft soul, young Graham," her father, Murdoch, once commented to Willow, "one that is guided by interference rather than direction. Don't interfere, Willow. It could be your downfall. Let the lad find his own way. He has to find his own path in life. It won't be too long before he leaves the mountain for university."

She never told Graham that she had visited Sir Jim. Sir Jim greeted her politely but never personally, and it was never mentioned again. What she did, she would have done again—with or without anyone's approval.

"Sorry I'm late," Graham called out to her as he walked down the cemetery path. "Sir Jim called me into his office. He said I can go back to my regular class on Monday."

"That's good news, Graham. What will your mother have to say about that?"

"I don't really care. I'll threaten to join the army in two years if she goes on and on."

"You better not join the army after all I—" Willow cut herself off before he questioned her.

"It's still what I want. I can't wait to get to university

and to see the world someday. I like big cities and I want to experience new cultures. I don't know why you're not thinking about university yourself. You're smarter than all of us. We could study together. We belong—"

Willow understood where his conversation was going. "I would go to university if I could sit on a window ledge and listen in like a crow. I'm not a crowd person and never will be."

She would not do anything to interfere with his dream. She was not his mother. He would go to university for seven years or more without interference. Or so she believed. She herself had not made any plans as of yet. She thought she might travel abroad with Marjorie and take in the Sistine Chapel in Rome and then follow up with a few art history courses while on her trip. Kiss the Blarney Stone in Ireland, maybe. She loved hanging upside down.

Willow ran her palm along Mary Ann MacIver's marble headstone. Kernels of moss collected in her hand and she rubbed them together until nothing remained but a stain on her skin. Perhaps the stain was an omen, one more thing she didn't believe in, for what was to come, and what was to go from her. Willow changed the mood of the conversation with Graham.

"I bet Mary Ann was one hell of a teacher. Can you imagine the stories she'd have to tell? She would have handled your mother with one hand."

"Or with one noose." Graham grinned back at her.

"Whatever works," Willow said. "Some say Mary Ann rode a wild stallion to school."

"Who really knows? I doubt it was possible for a teacher back then to get away with anything like that." Graham shrugged as he looked down at John Duncan's stone. "I hope he didn't suffer too much before he passed away. I think I would have liked this man."

‡ ‡ ‡

NOTHING WAS SAID when Graham returned to his regular class the following Monday. He smiled as he took his seat at the front of the room, near the doubled-paned window, where a crack in the right-hand corner of the glass was shaped like a horseshoe.

Marjorie gave him a stick of gum at recess.

Willow gave him a smile.

==

CHAPTER FIVE

The Drowning of Stones

N THE SUMMER BEFORE THEY ENTERED GRADE TEN, in 1960, Willow, Marjorie and Graham sat on the Glenmor wharf and threw stones into the sea.

"Let's each make a wish with our stones!" Willow said excitedly.

Graham's long legs dangled over the wharf. He splashed his feet into the cool water as he threw his stone towards a rolling wave. "Is this some ancient ritual?" he asked Willow.

"It could be, Graham," she replied without looking at him.

Marjorie was caught up in the secrecy and adventure of it all as she threw her stone a short distance.

Willow was the last to cast her stone. She stood on the edge of the wharf and swung high. The stone created a splash as it drowned in the sea. She was wearing cut-off jeans and a green cotton top. Under her clothes, her body moved like a snake in a silk sheet. Graham smiled as he watched her. He knew he was in for another sleepless night.

"When can we tell what we wished for?" Marjorie asked.

"It's like this, my friend. We will all meet here when we're sixty and reveal our wishes." Willow flashed a grin as she sat down beside Marjorie.

"Are you serious, Willow?" Marjorie sighed. "We could be long gone by then."

Graham smiled at Willow to assure her he'd be part of the revealing ritual. She smiled back. When they had arrived, a stretch of land could be seen across the harbour. Now a low bank of fog smothered the sea. The churning waves suddenly growled and shifted as they hit the side of the wharf.

"The tide is coming in." Graham's voice remained calm as he felt for his shoes. His hands moved swiftly. "We have to be careful of the waves."

Willow pulled Marjorie to her feet and shouted to Graham to hold on to her. Willow grabbed her other hand. Marjorie prayed aloud as they moved slowly along the planks.

"Our Father who art in heaven, we are too young to die."

Under the planks, the waves were rumbling, spitting up their froth through the cracks in the wharf. A salty, angry wave covered them like a dark quilt. It was Graham's idea to get down and crawl.

"We can move faster if we crawl," he called out. "And it's safer than standing when the waves hit."

They all stopped to get their balance. Marjorie had stopped praying out loud. She sealed her lips shut and began praying in her mind, as Graham pulled her down.

It was Willow who first noticed the dull searchlight coming from the lighthouse on the shore, moving lazily like a white moon, in and out of the clouds, scarring the darkness. The foghorn bellowed in through the wind like a rusty musician on a dead horn.

"We're near the shore," Willow cried as they edged their way to the damp sand under their knees.

Marjorie was both laughing and crying as she sat upright in the sand and gave thanks. Beautiful, petite Marjorie with her dark, straight hair pulled back into a braid. She was wearing her pedal-pushers and lucky rubber boots. Graham bent down and kissed Marjorie on the head. Willow promised Marjorie hot cocoa and toast when they got home, as if she were their child. Marjorie then watched as Graham pulled Willow shyly against his wet body. He smelled like the sea. She watched as Willow's mouth opened like a bird and waited for him to respond. Marjorie listened as Graham whispered to Willow: "I love you. I will always love you."

Marjorie waited for Willow's response. But Willow didn't say a word. Instead, she wrapped her arms around him and let him kiss her. Perhaps Willow's response was better than words. Marjorie was not quite sure what happened when people fell in love, but something bothered her as she watched them together. Her wish, from when she'd thrown her stone into the sea, lingered deep in her flesh like an invisible wound. Marjorie had wished that Willow would go to university with Graham. Anything could happen in seven years. At dances, girls circled him like flies. People changed. Marjorie was worried for them. And Willow was oblivious to it all.

Later, back at the house, when they were dry and snuggled under Willow's quilt, Marjorie asked Willow a question. "Why didn't you tell Graham that you loved him back, Willow?"

"Because I don't have to, Marjorie. I'm sure he knows. A girl doesn't always need words to get her message across. I kissed him. Didn't you see that?"

"But you're good with words. You always were. I think you will be a writer someday. The teachers always tell you how well you can write."

"Teachers aren't always right, Marjorie. Maybe I could be a writer if I could tell a story like your mother. I love her stories. Now go to sleep and stop worrying about love and who is in or out of it!"

"Willow, can you write me a story about scarecrows? My great-grandmother was French. She loved scarecrows as much as I do."

"Someday, Marjorie, but not tonight." Willow pulled the quilt up under her chin.

In five minutes, Marjorie was fast asleep, her dark hair winged against the white pillowcase, her breath floating softly in the air. The white moon found a spot on the window ledge beside her bed like a fat moth. Willow wrapped the quilt around her shoulders. Marjorie was right. She hadn't said "I love you" to Graham. She'd let him breathe his words into her. She opened her mouth and swallowed them whole.

Willow was a collector of words, and Marjorie's mother, Alma, helped set them free. Alma had six children ranging in age from three to ten when Willow first began going to their house. Marjorie, who was six at the time, took Willow to her home one Friday after school in 1951, and Alma welcomed her like one of her own. She grabbed Willow and held her in a bear hug against her gigantic breasts. Afterwards, Marjorie took Willow upstairs and they jumped in a mile-high haystack of clothes in the hallway.

"It's our closet," Marjorie said. "We can find anything we need to wear in here. We sniff around like hound dogs and Ma washes them out for us."

The four MacInnis girls slept in one bedroom and Marjorie's two brothers slung hammocks in the hall for beds. Their father worked on the docks, hundreds of miles away, in Halifax. When he came home, the kids would tear his kit bag from his back and sort out their treats. Then they'd follow him in a single line into the house, where a pot of stew and dumplings always awaited them. After meals, he took his fiddle from an old suitcase, well hidden under the bed in the downstairs bedroom, and began to play. His blue eyes twinkled like Christmas lights as he played. Everybody danced. The dishes were thrown into a large dishpan, drowned with a bucket of water and left to soak until morning. A grey mop was hung over the clothesline to bleach clean in the fog. When the kids fought, Marjorie's mother settled things down.

"All right, you hooligans, to the back of the truck. It's off to jail you go until you're old and grey!"

Willow anxiously watched for the next move. The children stood in a frozen line, scraps of pulled hair wrapped in their fists. Torn sleeves hung like dead skin. Dress hems floated over bare feet. Alma stood in the middle of the kitchen floor. Then she smiled and spread her massive pale arms and wrapped her warm, trembling flesh around her children.

"We love you, Ma," they mumbled in unison from under the smothering hug.

"And Ma loves her darlings," she replied, laughing.

Then they'd each slip from her grip one by one, faces flushed from fighting and fear. It was as though Alma had given birth, there in her dirty kitchen, to her beloved children once again. Afterwards, she'd sit them in a semicircle and read to them from *Grimm's Fairy Tales*. Sometimes she'd even make up stories of her own. These were the ones that captured Willow's imagination the most.

Willow was mesmerized by the scenes in Marjorie's home. She loved the chaos and merriment that blended their family. Until one day when everything came to a dark end and all was gone.

The MacInnis house caught fire and burned to the ground just as Willow, Graham and Marjorie had settled in to grade ten. The kids were all in school and their father was away, working on the docks. Alma was hanging out clothes and ran into the burning house to rescue the old fiddle. Afterwards, she picked the kids up from school, phoned her husband from her sister's house, and two days later left for Halifax with three of her children at her side. The other three were in the car behind her, being driven by her sister. Marjorie waved to Willow from the passenger window of the old truck as they drove away from Glenmor. Marjorie was wearing a blue dress and sweater given to her by Willow. In her arms she held her father's fiddle case.

Willow stood beside the road for a long time after they were out of sight. Then she turned and walked towards the blackened hole where Marjorie's old house once stood. She could still smell the smoke as she made the turn. Pieces of old boards rose from the ground like black arms reaching out to be saved. An old washer lay on its side, looking like a dead, fat seal washed up from the sea. Cast-iron headboards, three in a row, made a fence for the crows. In the centre of the black hole, the dishpan filled with broken dishes fired up small puffs of soot into the air. Willow's gaze rested on the heap of burnt rags near the blackened boards. She and Marjorie had rummaged through the "haystack" of clothes the day before the fire and found a red cardigan with a mallard duck on one of the pockets and a price tag dangling off the sleeve.

"My aunt sent it from the States," Marjorie had said. "You can have it. When I tried it on, I looked like the duck!"

Willow had thrown the sweater back on the pile. "I'll take it tomorrow."

There was one thing she could salvage, Willow thought. Below the old clothesline that had escaped the blaze, the grey mop lay on the ground. Willow picked up the mop and slung it over the clothesline and attached it with two clothespins. She would let some memories hang around. There had been little time for parting words, and too little time to finish the sentences that misfortune and sorrow had already written out. Willow's mother had the family over for supper the evening before they left, and she passed an envelope to Alma. A Bon Voyage card.

Willow watched her father walking towards her on the afternoon she went to see the ruins of Marjorie's home. On his face was a map of reality that only wise men travel.

"You must see this not as an ending, but as a new beginning for our friends. They will return one day, Willow," he said softly.

Murdoch Alexander wrapped his arm around his daughter's shoulder as they walked back towards the road. Willow thought of her father's words as she kicked a mound of small stones into the air. She believed her father. She always would.

CHAPTER SIX

==

The Next Step

Willow and Graham were eighteen years old and madly in love. Willow didn't like the expression "madly in love." Why couldn't people be mildly or quietly in love? Or "together by the force of chemistry that soon offered biology its path in the Garden of Eden"? But their days as carefree youngsters would soon come to an end. Graham would be off to Dalhousie University in Halifax to study medicine in the fall.

Willow's first plan was to go to St. Francis Xavier Junior College in Sydney to begin her Bachelor of Arts degree. Her great interest was art history, but she decided at the last minute to take a medical secretary course instead. The new doctor in the village, James Millhouse, was looking for a secretary. The course would be a benefit to her, she thought, when Graham returned and set up practice in Glenmor. By then she would have a few years under her belt and would be able to keep up with his work.

Graham had always been a healer. He had taken an interest in boils and misshapen limbs, fallen arches and weak hearts by the age of ten. He checked out roadkills and stared at a corpse longer than anyone else cared to examine death's stillness. As he got older, Graham was eager to become a licensed doctor. He worked hard and knew from a young age that he would climb the ladder that had not been available to his father. He took long walks with his father in the backwoods near their house. Graham smiled at the old stories his father told him. "Just between you and me, son, I always had a dream of owning a Model T. My buddy and me borrowed one from the old parish priest one night. Or rather stole it, because we didn't ask permission. It broke down near the Bent River, and that's where we left it and ran home through the back fields. It had run out of gas. Nobody knew it was ourselves that left it there. People believed it was the priest himself who got lost in his own memory of where he had been with the car."

Graham was the youngest of five and the only son. His sisters were much older than he was, and they were on their own. He would be the first to go to university—a boy from a poor family with a rich imagination.

On Graduation Day, Graham received a seven-year full scholarship to Dalhousie University. It was a scholarship from a company based in Halifax, the first one issued in the province of Nova Scotia. Graham smiled as he walked across the stage to receive his award from Sir Jim. Mrs. Currie screamed and had to be given two glasses of water to keep her from passing out. She had saved for only one year of tuition and had prayed for the rest.

Sir Jim was dressed in a grey, oversized striped suit and green tie. He jumped back a foot or more when he heard the scream. Graham reached for his elbow to balance him back on his sneakers that were hidden under the cuffs of his pants. Willow Alexander smiled. After the ceremony, Willow watched Graham stand beside his father. The meek, mild-mannered man regarded his son with pride. Graham put his arm around his father's shoulder for a photo. The old man slid a little forward, his face as grey as his hair. He knew what was to come for his son. He could hear his wife and daughters assaulting the crowds with Graham's success. His high marks. His future career. The large scholarship he had received. The money he'd make when he became a professional.

Graham's father took a deep breath and blew it out slowly. A slow glory swirled in the pit of his stomach. He felt at ease, because his son was free to live his own life, away from his mother's domineering nature and her displeasure with Willow Alexander, the girl Graham hoped to marry one day. Unlike his wife and daughters, Graham's father had always liked the young Alexander girl. He didn't believe, as they did, that Willow was proud, the way people with money get. He believed Willow and Graham would come back someday to the mountain to run his medical practice. He understood why Willow never left a footprint at his door. She was never welcomed.

When they assembled for a group photo—Willow and Graham and his parents—Mrs. Currie's tongue had not cooled down. Her target was too close.

"Graham," she said to her son, "aren't you the lucky one to be leaving the mountain to live on your own as a bachelor. Think of all the lovely women doctors you'll be surrounded by."

Willow felt Graham's arm stiffen under hers. She eyed the matriarch of madness in her purple dress. A grey lace scarf hung like a horse collar around her neck, collapsing over her large bosom. Her voice cracked like a whip as she turned to Willow.

"And what are your plans, Willow? I suppose you could enter the convent. The cloisters would be a good place for you. You would never have to speak again."

Willow eyed the woman. "No," she replied, "the convent is lost to me. I've been denied entry. They said I had to be a virgin. I was so disappointed to lose all that silence. I wish I'd kept my mouth closed, and the rest of me too."

Willow watched as Mrs. Currie's pointed bosom heaved like seals' heads in a grey wave. Foam covered her lips. Her head wobbled. She reached for a rebuttal, but her words were drowned in the foam. Instead, she spit into a tissue.

Her three daughters formed a posse around her and led her out of the hall. Her husband walked behind them with a wicked smile on his face. It was the first time Willow had ever seen the man smile.

Graham's face, however, was ashen. He shook his head in slow motion. "Do you understand what this means, Willow?"

"Who cares?"

"I care, Willow. She'll do anything to get back at you."

"What's she going to do? Phone the university and tell them you're not a virgin and have you expelled? And then shoot me?"

"She could go to your parents and tell them what you said."

"She wouldn't dare. I know her type. She won't mention it again. She'd never face my father. I never liked her, and she's never liked me. End of story, Graham."

Willow grabbed Graham by the arm as the celebration music started and pulled him close to her. Flashbulbs popped. The graduating class of Juniper High School started dancing. Balloons floated down over the students from a net on the ceiling before bursting over the crowd like gunshots. Willow lifted her head over Graham's shoulder to look at the entrance, checking to see if Mrs. Currie had returned.

A full moon traced the outline of the school. Some of the parents blew their car horns as they drove out of the parking lot after the ceremony and left the students to their night of celebrations and dancing. Willow stepped out a side door into warm breeze. She was elated for Graham. She whispered a silent thank-you under her breath.

The thank-you was for her maternal grandfather, Sid Cropper. Sid's face floated before her—his bald head tilted, his round, pale face and his double chin below a weak smile evaporating in a passing mist. The image of him was from his wedding photo, where he looked as though he was listening intently to his bride, Edith. What had he longed to hear? The judge, who lay down the gavel on the law of others, had married the woman who stood before him without judgment, while his immediate family made no appearance on this day. They heard nothing of the vows he made to love and obey the delicate needle-and-thread woman beside him. Her grandmother looked as though her vows had been unrehearsed—a spur-of-the-moment commitment to the man whose sudden death kept her a widow for the rest of her life.

Long dead, the couple would never know that their granddaughter, Willow, whom they never met, was remembering them at such an important moment as this. Willow knew that her mother, who inherited considerable wealth from her father, had generously shared her fortune in secrecy. And at this moment, young Graham Currie was unaware of his benefactor. Willow wanted to keep the secret about her grandfather and how his money had provided aid to so many. She thought Judge Sid Cropper would have agreed. He looked like a man whose secrets were hidden like wounds that never break the skin. She knew and believed something else about the legacy Sid Cropper left behind: he loved a beautiful woman and an ugly dog.

==

CHAPTER SEVEN

Money and Magic Wands

WILLOW'S MOTHER, RHONA, WAS THE ONLY child of Edith and Sid Cropper. Rhona had been conceived but had yet to be born when Judge Sid Cropper suffered his fatal heart attack. Edith was pregnant with Rhona when she returned from Boston after her husband died. She felt she would be safer in Glenmor, her village, with a small child to raise. She never remarried.

As a young girl, Rhona slept in a pink room with long white starched curtains on a window that looked out to the mountains. Whenever she awoke from a bad dream, she believed she was in the presence of ghosts, as white forms floated over her bed in waves of lace.

Edith played on young Rhona's innocence, believing that she was comforting her fears as she blindly fumbled for the magic ghost wand she kept under her bed whenever the hysterical Rhona ran into her room in the middle of the night. Edith questioned her about the ghosts.

"Did one of them look like your father?" her mother asked.

"I don't know what my father looked like," the child sobbed.

"You know what the ghosts looked like, don't you?"

"They were all white, Mommy, coming through my open window. They didn't have any heads."

"I showed you your father's picture many times. He was a fat man with a bald head and an ugly dog."

"Can your magic wand get rid of him, please?"

It was rumoured that ghosts valued the real estate along the Bent River at Glenmor, where the white bones of Willow's ancestors lay melting in the winter frost in the Journey's End Cemetery below the mountain. The black wrought iron cemetery gates opened without a squeak to the living and the dead, where believers and atheists settled a foot or two apart in shrinking slumber.

Up and down the cemetery paths, without supervision, Rhona strolled as a young child with her English pram and her twin dolls, Rory and Ruby. She was told ghosts do not appear in the light, so she felt safe.

"Ghosts have vision problems in the daylight, just like bats," her mother assured her.

But Rhona tucked the ghost wand under her twins in the pram, just in case. The paths were well-groomed in the cemetery and free of the dirt and gravel that collected in the wheels of her pram on the country roads.

Rhona had no way of knowing that seeds of anxiety were already sprouting in her young mind as she held hands with death and magic at the end of a stick. She could not comprehend why or how her father could arrive for a friendly visit through her window without a head and could be escorted out with the swish of a magic ghost wand like a blue-tail fly.

Edith, a kind but naive woman, revealed very little to Rhona about her father, the man she had met in a park walking his overweight dog. The mutt was homely, with a dropped snout and eyes the colour of mustard. He answered to the name of Brutus. Edith had written home that she was fond of Sid Cropper from the get-go, although she was afraid of Brutus, who seemed attached to Sid's heels. Sid's mother's family was wealthy. Eldora Cropper owned a coffee company in Colombia, her native home. But her husband was British, and she enjoyed a good cup of tea daily at three in the afternoon. "Not a biscuit in sight, though," Edith had silently remarked to herself when she visited Sid's parents. She was used to tea biscuits and date squares with her tea.

Whenever Rhona thought about her father in the years that followed, his image came to her like a dark umbrella over her head, faceless and voiceless in scattered dreams that left a pounding in her head. She would bolt upright from sleep and check her sealed windows, ensuring nothing flew by. Rhona looked nothing like the Cropper family. And since not one of them attempted to make any connection with her or her mother, she gave them very little thought except for the photos her mother gave her as a keepsake to glance at now and then.

"They are your family, Rhona," her mother had muttered. "And even though you'll never get to see a hair on their heads, their blood is running through your veins. There's no doubt you would have loved your father. Bald or not, he was a fine man. Always good and kind to me."

One summer, Edith went to Boston to visit her sister, and Rhona was alone in the house when a crackly phone call came in the middle of the night that terrified her. When she picked up the phone, her aunt's frantic voice shouted into the receiver, "Rhona, dear, your mother's taken ill. They say there's bleeding in her brain. She's in and out of the fog of Cape Breton one minute and strolling the streets of Boston the next. We think you should come soon!"

A week later, Edith Cropper was buried beside her husband, Sid. When Rhona read the headstone, she learned something about her father she had not known before: his second name was Henry. Sidney Henry Cropper.

A sprinkle of relatives Rhona had never met gathered in dark suits and gloves at the gravesite. They observed eighteen-year-old Rhona as a foreigner in her pleated tartan skirt and white blouse, as if she might have been a girl who'd missed her flight to Scotland. They shook hands with her without removing their gloves. They spoke very few words.

After the final prayer, as the casket sank slowly into the ground past Sid's gavel, her mother's sister whispered in her ear: "Pay no attention to them, Rhona. They're city people."

Sid's sisters who attended the funeral were large-boned women in black tailored suits, meaty, weathered females who wore horn-rimmed glasses harnessed to the bridge of their nose, with eyes the colour of rusty tin cans. Willow spliced these images together from the naive tales her mother had told her about the Croppers. She imagined their family tree being pulled by Clydesdales, strong, sturdy horses capable of hauling the Cropper weight. How had they perceived poor Edith, with her delicate hands and fine features? She had been a seamstress in a fashionable bridal shop, who dressed in pastel colours—a pale collision with her two "successful" sisters-in-law, both criminal lawyers, and their sombre attire.

Their mother, Eldora, had run the coffee business while her husband drank dark rum on ice. In a back room with the door bolted, the girls smoked cigars, which were said to have come from Fidel Castro himself, a cousin of their late mother, who often spoke Spanish to them while they smoked when they were young. There were no official documents or photos to imply that the Cropper sisters held any sympathies with Fidel; it was simply hearsay. They were known to be brilliant, argumentative and demanding, and were both feared and admired. They avoided long conversations with Edith and did not attend the wedding of their only brother but appeared at Edith's funeral to sniff out Sid's offspring. They looked for family resemblances in Rhona's drawn face, her green eyes. They found no real evidence of the strong Cropper stock, they said. No meat on her bones for a good defence. Too delicate for a weighty career. She belonged to a thread-and-needle life, like her mother. There was, however, one stamp of Cropper evidence they all observed in Rhona: a bold, exasperated twist on her lip.

There were also cousins who attended the funeral. They entertained each other in Spanish and laughed out loud during the burial. Her grandparents, Rhona believed, were no longer living.

A few weeks later, Rhona returned to Cape Breton as the beneficiary of her mother's estate of over one million dollars. The first thing the frugal Rhona purchased, at a discounted price, was a generous supply of watercolours and oils.

CHAPTER EIGHT

Mutiny on the Mountain

WILLOW REMOVES AN OLD ALBUM FROM A drawer in the table beside the sofa. She takes the Croppers from its pages and stacks them on the sofa in a heap. Old Grandma Cropper looks up at her from sepia-coloured snake eyes. Sid's father is caught in a haze of smoke leaning over a wooden desk, reaching for a bottle of dark rum. He is missing a few teeth, but his smile is as wide as a saucer. In the next photo are her two aunts, Sid's sisters, the lawyers, all dressed in black. Dark shadows against a brick wall, they carry briefcases like machine guns, tight and firm against their bodies. There's another image of Sid, playing with his dog on a beach. The dog is digging a hole as though he plans on burying poor Sid's bones for safekeeping. The hole looks deep enough to bury his body whole. Did the dog know something Sid did not?

How little she knows of her maternal relatives has weighed heavily on her over the passing years. Willow contemplates the two Cropper sisters against the brick wall. Why had they remained so elusive to their only brother? For once she wished she had met the Croppers. She wondered what had attracted Sid and Edith to each other. Was beauty the trade-off for money? They looked happy in their photo. And why had her grandmother Edith never remarried?

Willow tries to imagine the Croppers in Glenmor in the winter. Snowed in with not a cigar or bottle of rum for miles. Not a courthouse in sight, and poor Brutus terrified by coyotes. It makes her smile to think of the Croppers with their guard down. There might have been a mutiny on the mountain. Money couldn't have freed them from a blizzard.

Willow makes her way to the kitchen stove. She opens the lid and cremates the rest of the Croppers in one intense blue flame, keeping only Sid and his dog. She observes the grey ashes descend beneath the grate and curl against each other. She wonders what has taken her so long to rid herself of all the Cropper photos. They served no purpose in her memory.

Willow returns to the parlour and flips open the album of her and Graham. There is a photo of him smiling up at her in his high school graduation cap and gown. She had suggested that day that he keep his mouth closed for the picture.

"Why?" Graham had asked.

"Your front teeth. One is longer than the other."

"Your nose is longer than mine, Willow," Graham had replied. "Do you intend to cut a piece off your nose for our wedding picture?"

She closes the album on the smiling faces of herself and Graham. Willow is finished with the photos for now. She cannot destroy these photos. She needs these reminders to keep her anger going.

CHAPTER NINE

The Announcement

AS YOUNGSTERS, WILLOW AND GRAHAM PLAYED hide-and-seek in the cemetery, behind the tallest tombstones, the ones with an edge at the bottom of the marble base wide enough to sit on. She always won. They took inventory of the dead who gave them rest, and knew their full names and dates of birth and death. They knew whom they married and when. The daughters and sons of the first settlers of Glenmor and beyond became like lost family members. They referred to the cemetery as their social history class.

It was here that Graham proposed to Willow just before he left for university. His plan was to set up practice in Glenmor and have Willow as his assistant. She said yes to his marriage proposal while leaning against the tombstone of spinster Mary Ann MacIver. Willow believed the fantasy, standing above the dead that autumn, leaves tumbling and curling before their own demise. Red squirrels flew in and out of trees as quick as fire. Sharp as a blade of frost came the wind through the white maples. Life flowed smoothly in Glenmor's graveyard when Willow and Graham committed themselves to a future together.

While he was away, they talked on the phone. Willow visited him often. Two years before graduating from medical school, Graham came home for a visit. His father was ill, and he was eager to get back to the mountain for good.

"A life for us, Willow," Graham said as they walked along the sea. "You and me in a log home, wrapped up together on cold winter nights. What more does a man need?"

Whenever he came home, they climbed like mountain goats. On the highest peak the moon found their love nest, while a waterfall screamed in the distance. They were liberal thinkers. He used protection, stolen from the hospital to keep their loving safe.

Willow kept their plans a secret. They felt no need to whisk their future into the ear of anyone else. She did tell Marjorie, though, before asking her to be her maid of honour. Willow casually announced their marriage plans to everyone else six weeks before the wedding, as though she were planning a new hairdo.

There was a lot to be done before the wedding, and Marjorie arrived back in Glenmor two weeks in advance to help Willow prepare. Willow's mother made her wedding dress and cake. Everyone in the town was invited, as was the marriage custom in Glenmor. The community hall was booked for receptions by Willow's father, who was caretaker of the hall. Willow wanted to pick wildflowers for her bouquet just before she went to the church, daisies full of summer sunshine surrounded by baby's breath. She wanted everything still breathing on her special day.

Rhona and Murdoch went to visit the Currie family to invite them to participate in the wedding arrangements. Willow's parents were met at the door by Mrs. Currie and were not invited in past the mat.

"This is your affair, not ours," Mrs. Currie hissed. "I see no need for a Currie nose to smell what money can offer. My family will not be in attendance. This is your feast, it's not something we Curries could afford."

There was a loud crash from somewhere inside the house, as though something had been thrown against a wall. Mr. Currie coughed loudly. Rhona tried to repeat the invitation but felt her hand being tugged lightly by her husband. Murdoch offered Mrs. Currie a polite "Good day" and walked off the step with his wife in tears.

"This is terrible for Graham," Rhona wept. "I wanted to say something impolite to her for his sake. And his father—I know he would want to be at his son's wedding."

Murdoch remained stoic as he looked at his wife. "You were right to keep your silence, dear. When you confront the enemy, you become one yourself."

"What should we do, Murdoch? People will talk. Graham will be hurt. I know he will want his father there."

"We'll do and say nothing more. What others say is of no concern to us. I'm sure Graham's father knows he's very welcome to attend. I know he heard our conversation."

After lunch on the Saturday before the wedding, Marjorie and Willow walked down to Marjorie's old homestead under sturdy umbrellas. A soft rain danced in the puddles at their feet.

"I'm going to rebuild here, Willow. I want to live here again," Marjorie said as she surveyed the vacant hole that was once the fortress of the MacInnis clan. "I miss the chaos of a large family. Ma and Da can't wait to move back to the mountains. We plan to build a 'granny suite' on the house so they can have their privacy. I plan to use the life insurance to rebuild the house. It's hard to believe, Willow, that I'm already a widow." Marjorie took a deep breath. "Oliver was a good husband in many ways. You warned him that smoking two packs of cigarettes a day would do him in. I'm glad I didn't divorce Oliver when we parted. He died two months later."

Willow sighed. "I hope Graham has quit smoking. I warned him too."

"Oliver said he smoked too much because I talked too much. I told him talking doesn't kill people. But I was too young to get married, Willow. At twenty, marriage should only be a noun, not a nuptial."

Willow laughed.

"I must have thought the smoke was passion mist. You

never know what love can make a fool think or do. We eloped. That was a crazy idea."

"I know, Marge. You *did* invite me to the elopement."

The girls shared a hearty laugh.

"Give me a fisherman any day or night. I can tolerate the smell of fish. I want a family. I hope you and Graham have a half-dozen kids to play with mine."

Willow eyed her friend. "Why don't you make a play for the best man? He's a fisherman, and he's single. You remember Colin? From Baddeck."

"You know how much I always wanted to teach here in the mountains, Willow. I'll have to wait. It will be another two years before I get my teacher's degree." Marjorie grinned. "I'll give him the eye for sure, and we'll see if he takes the bait." Marjorie wrapped her arms around Willow. "Graham must be over the moon, Willow. And your parents must be so happy."

A kink in Willow's quiet smile caught Marjorie's attention. She posed her question delicately to Willow. "Is everything okay with you and Graham? I've seen happier faces on a corpse."

Willow eyed Marjorie. "My parents told me the Curries will not be attending the wedding. I'm heartbroken."

Then they broke into peals of laughter again.

"Can you imagine Graham's sisters missing their brother's wedding, Willow?" Marjorie snorted, holding her side.

Willow caught her breath. "I suspect there'll be Currie

noses hiding in the trees somewhere to get a glimpse of everyone, don't you worry. The old woman will need a play-by-play . . . or maybe she'll be up in a tree too!"

The girls' laughter burst out once again. But a sadness crossed Willow's face. "I really feel sad for Graham's father, though, Marge. I plan to tell Graham to make sure his father is there in church with him."

"Have you told Graham that his mother and sisters won't be there?"

"Yes, I did, and his response was strange: he said maybe he wouldn't show up either. But not having his family involved made the entire wedding much easier to arrange. I think he's been working too hard, and I told him not to come home until the rehearsal."

"His response was obviously a joke," Marjorie said.

"I don't know, Marge. He's been quiet the last few weeks, like someone undone. At first, I really wanted him to come home this weekend so that we could all celebrate together. I know I shouldn't have changed my mind about that, telling him to stay in Halifax and catch some rest."

"Why isn't he here, Willow? He should've come back here if he needed a rest," Marjorie quizzed.

"It's the same old excuse. Some doctor wants him to do some research. He said he needs the money for the wedding and the doctor pays very well."

"Is this person male or female?" Marjorie laughed. "Did he say?"

Willow starved off a laugh. "Are you kidding, Marjorie? She's an older woman."

"Yes, I'm kidding. And I'm hungry. Let's get back to the house for supper!"

‡ ‡ ‡

LATER THAT EVENING, Rhona measured Marjorie for her maid of honour gown. "I'll get started on your dress tonight. I drew up the pattern before you arrived."

"Thanks so much. It looks beautiful, Rhona." Marjorie beamed.

"Willow, try on your gown for Marjorie. There are still a few seams I want to tuck in." Rhona's voice was anxious. She did not want to miss a stitch.

"Come on, Willow," Marjorie prodded. "I can't wait to see you in all your glory. Put on your gown, my friend!"

Marjorie heard the soft sound of satin as it slid down over Willow's white flesh, over the thickening mound just below her waist, that gentle bump that her hand circled around. Someone she caresses who will one day caress her back. Someone who will wait with her when Graham is too busy at work.

Marjorie knew her friend's secret. Good friends just know these things. But Marjorie had remained silent. She knew Willow had kept her secret just for Graham. She knew Willow wanted Graham to be the first to know. She hadn't given him the news yet. Marjorie would not mention a word. This was Willow's news to tell.

There was an air of quiet sadness in the room. Marjorie inhaled it. The air was too still. The sky had broken into scrambled egg clouds outside the window. The rain had stopped. Rhona threaded her needle with a shaking hand. Marjorie noticed her troubled hand and the time it took her to tie the knot on the end of the thread. Perhaps it was nerves or excitement, or she was concerned about the old wives' tale.

"You should take the gown off before I stitch it, Willow. It could be bad luck. I know where the troubled spots are now." Rhona recited out loud, "'Stitch a person with clothes on their back, and life will give them an awful whack.'"

Willow stood still in the middle of the room and smiled quietly. "What could go wrong?" She was beautiful and radiant, with Graham's gift growing under her satin, waiting to be tucked in, here and there, as her mother's needle found the seams and slipped in as quietly as a poem.

A ray of sunlight entered the opened window. It found Willow in the middle of the room and coasted slowly through her damp curls, picked up speed down the bodice of her elegant gown, over the hidden bump, then slid down the skirt, spraying it a vibrant golden colour before it disappeared as quickly as it had entered. Willow smiled as she reached out to touch her mother's hand.

She turned towards Marjorie, who was dancing with joy around the room now. "Willow, you are a vision of Celtic fire, woman," Marjorie exclaimed. She joined Willow's warm laughter.

"You've always had the right words for any occasion, my friend Marjorie."

"You're pulling my leg, Willow."

"Not at all. In fact, I believe I will give you my special gift for being my maid of honour. Tomorrow. You can hang it on the wall of your new house when it's ready."

Willow removed a painting wrapped in silver paper from the trunk at the foot of her bed. Marjorie unravelled it carefully and slowly.

"Remember how you've always wanted me to write something for you. Voilà."

Marjorie's eyes widened. She wept openly and genuinely over the painting. "My grandmother's scarecrows. You titled them *The Ambassadors of the Fields*. I love it."

"My mother drew the scarecrows and I supplied a short version of the story I wrote for you," Willow explained. "The full story is in the envelope taped to the painting."

I remember them clearly now being taken from their dusty hibernation: they without voices, they without sight, they without protest, sent out into the world to guard and protect in mute, turbulent splendour, the reason for their being.

I had watched their birth in my grandfather's barn. Bijou first, created with the rugged alertness that appears on the faces of the already damned. And Seline, his mate, kindly with a radiant sadness. Leaning side by side in their assembled nakedness, they caught their first glimpse of each other.

A scarecrow stood on either side of the verse. Marjorie was overwhelmed by the painting. "How can you make two pieces of wood come to life like that, Willow? They seem real to me."

"How can you make anything come to life, Marjorie? My mother is very upset that Graham's people are not going to attend the wedding. Is it because they're made of wood? No. It's his mother. She believes she is the only woman who can do anything for him. She lives through him. She was the first woman to kiss his handsome face and she wanted to be the last. Take a good look at Mrs. Currie's face and see what appears on the face of the already damned!"

CHAPTER TEN

—

Premonition

THE FOLLOWING WEEK, MARJORIE AND WILLOW ran into Mrs. Currie and two of her daughters at the general store. Marjorie held on to Willow's arm as Mrs. Currie rambled on to the shopkeeper about Graham's fine grades.

"I can't say he is anxious to come home. He's working for a doctor doing research for a book. That's what people who study and work at the same time can achieve for themselves."

"That's right, Ma," the two sisters added in unison as they looked around the store to see whose ear they had caught.

The storekeeper, well aware that commerce is more valuable than insults, greeted Willow with a smile. She made a mental note of the wealth Rhona Alexander had dropped on her counter over the years. Rhona was her best customer by far.

"How is the bride-to-be?" she chirped at Willow. "I'll be there at the church with bells on, come Saturday."

Willow thanked the storekeeper just as the shop door slammed shut. The Curries had made a quick exit, leaving behind several flying splinters from the wooden door.

That evening, Graham phoned Willow to apologize for not coming down on the weekend. "Willow, I'm tied up in knots here. I'd much rather be in Glenmor with you. Sometimes I wish I'd never left."

"I know you're busy, Graham. I heard your mother talking about the extra work you took on for that doctor. I didn't realize you had told your mother."

"I mentioned it to my father. She must have overheard the conversation. Will that woman ever let things go?" Graham sighed. "One of these days she's going to see the light, and I hope you'll be there to watch it flashing."

"What about the woman you're doing research work for? Does she plan on coming to the wedding?"

Graham hesitated before he answered, then began to ramble nervously. "I don't think so. I told you before, she's an older woman. Heavy into research. Pays very well. I'll be home Friday before the wedding rehearsal. I'll see you then." And he quickly said his goodbye.

There were three things in that phone conversation with Graham that Willow didn't question. She didn't ask about the woman's voice in the background that called out his name. Women's voices are everywhere. Another woman's voice was never a threat to Willow.

She didn't question the hesitation and nervousness in Graham's voice. He knew what his mother had said when Willow's parents went to her door. He was no doubt embarrassed by it all.

And she didn't question how anxious he was to end the phone call with her. It wasn't a problem for Willow, since she wasn't a phone person. She and Graham would have years together to talk.

But Marjorie knew something was off-kilter. The old Graham would have been home a week ago helping out. Marjorie remained silent. Was something wrong? Should she mention something to her friend? It was a delicate situation. She suspected Murdoch Alexander had analyzed it all already. Marjorie couldn't go to Rhona either, because she would be convinced that she had caused the problems with an ill-timed needle and thread, bringing down a curse upon her daughter's head.

CHAPTER ELEVEN

=

The Introduction of Deceit

THE INTRODUCTION OF POLINA REBANE AND Graham Currie had been an awkward one. It happened two and a half months before Willow and Graham were to become man and wife. Graham had watched Polina's long, dangling limbs struggle between chairs in the hospital cafeteria—she had upset two of them—as she made her way to the empty chair beside him at his table.

"Is this chair safe?" asked Polina, flushed.

"For now," Graham answered. "It's still on its four legs."

Polina appeared neither embarrassed nor amused as she sat down and crossed her legs. She had the kind of vacant face that employed no wit. Her dark eyes were small and serious as she focused on Graham Currie's handsome face. An aching determination blinked behind her lids. She was not a pretty woman, not even remotely attractive. Her only notable attribute was her soft, pale skin, which was like a child's face shattered with rain, damp, pink and flawless, and desperately in need of a smile.

"What's your name?" she asked, though she already knew it. But she wanted to hear what else his deep voice had to offer, how he phrased each word from his shapely mouth. She had spent considerable time researching the handsome young man in front of her.

"I'm Graham Currie. I'm a resident here."

"You're a Scot."

"Not full-blooded. My mother is Acadian French."

Polina Rebane frowned. "You must have had one combative upbringing." She folded her arms across her flat chest. "I'm Polina Rebane, a Harvard graduate. I'm an orthopaedic surgeon from New York. I'm thirty years old. An only child of two angry parents who wanted no offspring. My father called my birth a mistake of the loins. My mother discovered his mistake too late to put an end to it." Polina turned quickly to look at something or someone behind her. She checked every corner of the room as though she were checking out a surveillance order.

"My parents are doctors from the Baltics," she continued as she turned towards Graham. "They put me in a boarding school when I was seven. I started medical school at an early age. Now I am in Nova Scotia to do research on a book I'm writing on bones. I have a publisher in New York waiting for my first draft."

Graham looked over at the two tumbled chairs, a pair of folded arms and a pair of legs crossed like scissors, and felt he was under surveillance of some sort. "Why are you telling me all this?" he asked. "I'm sure there are plenty of bones to research in New York."

"I've heard good things about you, Dr. Currie, from some of the older docs here."

"What do you want me to do for you, Dr. Rebane?" Graham asked the eccentric woman at his table who he believed would never leave.

"You can start by calling me Polina."

"Polina, I am very busy at the moment. I have a wedding planned and at this moment my wife-to-be is very busy getting everything arranged. We will live here in Halifax until I am finished with university and all."

Polina interrupted him. "One day, when I marry, my parents will offer me a clinic in New York as a wedding gift. You, Graham Currie, belong in a big city, with big opportunities. Not here. Your brain is too hungry to stay in such an undernourished city."

Polina offered a large sum of money to Graham Currie to help her with her research. "I am writing a book on bones, and I need help with my research. Your name came up in conversations with a highly respected doctor here. I will pay you very well indeed. I've already received a down payment for the research grant," she added.

Graham didn't reply too quickly. He could overlook

her vain approach to life as something most needy people require. Yet he realized he would have to be wary of her motives and her forward approach. He certainly could use the money to help out with the costs of the wedding attire he would need.

A week later, Graham accepted Polina's offer with conditions. His personal life came first, he told her firmly—his wife and career.

Polina invited him to dinner one evening to go over the details of the project. On the table, a red candle rose as sturdy as a rooster's neck at dawn. Beside the candle, a bottle of the finest Irish whiskey sucked in the flame, its dark liquid sluggish and thick like a vein ready to burst from the heat. Two wineglasses stood nearby on the bare table; Polina didn't have whiskey glasses. Graham handed her a hundred typed pages of research notes he had put together. She didn't turn a page to check for errors. Instead, she opened the whiskey and poured Graham a full glass and one for herself.

"Drink up!" she growled like a tormented cat. "Take two or three sips before you swallow!"

He watched her face over the rim of his glass.

"You must never dilute fine whiskey, my friend. Believe me, its strength is its pleasure."

Graham took a long hard drink of the whiskey. He moved slowly across the kitchen and rescued the saucepan from the stove, dropped the smoking pan into a sink full of water and took another gulp of whiskey. Polina began to sway, with the whiskey in one hand and seduction in her eyes. Graham took another drink. He was not a drinking man. The room was spinning like a wheel. His head felt heavy. He reached for his jacket on the back of a chair. He needed fresh air desperately and wanted to get away and end their deal before it continued any further.

Polina was within touching distance of him now. He stepped back. He didn't want her too close to him. He knew what Polina had planned. His legs folded like rubber beneath him. He stumbled as she reached out to him and led him towards her unmade bed of cold, wrinkled sheets. "You need to rest awhile. You've had too much to drink," was the last thing he recalled her saying to him.

Graham woke up in the morning with a dead memory in a dirty bedroom. Polina was sleeping soundly beside him. They were both naked. He grabbed his muddled clothes off the floor and made his way to the kitchen. The front of his shirt was ripped open. Buttons sprawled like broken teeth along a trail leading to her bedroom. Graham made his way quietly through the kitchen and out the front door of the apartment building. The sidewalk was empty, and he stopped and rested his back against the cool cement of a foundation. His head felt as if it were splitting in two, as though an axe were lodged in his skull. A black alley cat moved slowly towards him.

"Frig off," Graham cried out in pain and misery at the approaching animal.

The cat inched closer to him.

"Go away!" Graham screamed at the cat again.

The cat hissed.

Graham remembered a stick of salami he'd shoved into his back pocket in the cafeteria the day before. The cat's head jerked up as it caught the smell in the air. Graham held a small bite in his hand. He watched as the animal jumped into his lap and devoured the meat. Then the cat's teeth sank into his palm and it ran its coarse tongue along his bloody hand and licked its lips. The alley cat sat in Graham's lap and purred. Graham touched its mangled fur. Its ribs protruded in places. Scars ran along its skin like amateur tattoos. The cat was no doubt a scrapper, who took its wins and losses in downtown alleys.

"I wish I could live life like you," Graham said to the cat. "I hate myself, even though I can't remember anything that happened last night."

The cat yawned. Dug its head under Graham's chin and lapped up the salt in the tears that rolled down his face.

The cat eyed Graham as though it understood his agony. What Graham Currie had done was very little. Polina Rebane was asleep as soon as she hit her cold sheets. He had not touched her as she had planned, for she was in love with him. Instead, she fell into a dream that foretold her future with Graham for the next ten years. In the dream, she watched their wedding in black and white. He gave her his grandmother's wedding ring and refused to smile.

She didn't care. Very few people smiled at her anyway. She never drew anyone's attention. Her mind was her weapon. She had no publisher for her research in New York. She had seduced Graham with the lie of a publisher to get him into her bed.

Now Graham was forced to confront the fact that he had lost his self-respect and his self-worth by allowing himself to give in to her offer of a job. He had no reason to accept the liquor; he was not a drinking man. He could have survived financially without taking on Polina Rebane's research money. He felt like a man at the gallows who is pardoned at the final hour but is never free. He had placed his poverty-stricken morals ahead of his love for Willow. He knew his life with Willow Alexander was now over. She was too good for him. He didn't deserve her. How could he marry someone like her without confessing the truth? He could never tell Willow what he had done to make money for their wedding. The idea of his behaviour would be revolting to her. He had one victory he could maintain for himself: to achieve his medical degree to please the woman he left behind.

Two months previously, Graham had spent the night with Willow in her hotel room in Halifax. He made love to her like a man going off to war. Through the window, a pale comma of a moon found them lying on the bed in their naked expectations of the future. He caressed her sturdy body and held her firmly in his arms, letting his hands swim down to the ripples in her long calves. They talked about their wedding plans and where they would live before he could open up his own practice. And they decided on his return date to Glenmor.

Weeks later, he phoned Willow to tell her that he was doing extra work for the doctor, helping her research a book she was writing. His voice quivered. He needed the extra money, he explained, for his expenses.

"You sound weary, Graham." She caught the sadness in his voice. "Perhaps you're taking on too much extra work."

"I'm okay, Willow. I'll see you soon. I just got in from the hospital."

"I think you should stay in Halifax and rest up before the big day, Graham. Everything is pretty well set here. Marjorie is arriving next week. We'll be busy setting things up. My dress is ready. My mother is calling to me from the bottom of the stairs, Graham. I have to go. I believe some-one is at the door with some delivery or other."

And then she hung up.

═

CHAPTER TWELVE

Satin Flames

G RAHAM CURRIE MADE ONE FINAL VISIT TO
Glenmor. It was on a Friday, when he came home
for the wedding rehearsal.

There were only a few people in the church. He stood
at the front with his friend and best man, Colin. Graham
watched as his beloved Willow walked up the aisle.
Marjorie walked ahead of her and joined Colin. Nobody
smiled as they took their places. Willow was wearing a
light-green dress and jacket to match. Her hands were at
her side. Murdoch Alexander stood close beside his daughter. Marjorie kept her head down as her tears fell. Willow
and Graham stood side by side at the foot of the altar, so
close to their happy ending, so far from their beginning.
They were given their instructions by the priest for their
big day, the next morning. Willow's face glowed. Graham
had not shaved, and his hair was uncombed. The sharp

pain of betrayal wrinkled his brow. Why had he made such a rumpled spectacle of himself? And why was Willow so accepting of his appearance (a question that would haunt her for years)? He looked like a scarecrow who had been out in the field too long.

Graham felt vomit swimming up to his throat. He took deep breaths. His heart raced under his wrinkled shirt.

He listened to the priest's instructions, yet he didn't hear a word. Having Willow so close to him was almost unbearable. He prayed silently, "Lord Jesus Christ, help me!" Graham looked towards the crucified Christ hanging above the altar, His head tilted forward, His eyes sunken into death. Graham could feel his own body breaking. He was having a panic attack. Behind him, Willow's father took in his every move. Murdoch knew the young man about to marry his daughter was very, very troubled.

Graham held Willow's hands before he left the church, struggling with the last few words he spoke to her. "I will always love you," he said. Then he was gone.

Willow had felt the tension in his hands. Nerves, she told herself as she mouthed the words back to him in silence.

Graham didn't remember leaving the church that day, or Colin driving him back to his car, parked a few miles from the church. Colin remained silent. He knew there would be no wedding in the morning. Graham did not tell him the reason; he simply said it would not be taking place. His friend shook his hand before leaving.

"If you need to talk, Graham," Colin said softly, "give me a call."

Murdoch Alexander regretted not stopping Graham as he ran from the church. He should have had a man-to-man talk with him. He should have asked to meet Graham in private somewhere. He could tell Graham was falling apart. What would he have said to him? Would Graham have opened up to his future father-in-law, a man he highly respected? Murdoch would have understood the torments of a man who had introduced himself to darkness. Graham was a good man, but he was a man. Honest and gifted, though he'd be easily chosen to take a fall. Murdoch could have settled Graham Currie's conscience in one conversation. He would have suggested that Willow be informed. And then he would have gone to Graham's supervisor with him and had him tell his story. He would have had no doubt that he was telling the truth.

As it happened, Graham drove by the Alexander house twice that night to see if there was a light on in Murdoch's work shed. He wanted desperately to speak to him. When he saw the shed outlined in darkness, Graham dropped his head against the cool steering wheel of his car. He couldn't knock on the Alexanders' front door. It was too late.

Inside the darkness of the work shed, a mouse rummaged through a pile of wood shavings. It chewed and clawed its way, looking for a morsel of relief, but it found nothing in its blind search. It was being watched, and it died on an empty stomach. The feral cat, locked in the shed, did not require a light to trap its victim.

Graham backed out from under the small grove of trees and began his trip back to the city. He eased the car out onto the narrow road that led away from Willow's door and didn't look back until Christy's Mountain, and Glenmor, were long gone behind him.

‡ ‡ ‡

THE NEXT MORNING, on Willow and Graham's almost-wedding day, Murdoch Alexander drove home from the church with Rhona beside him, silenced by fear and deep sadness for their daughter. In the back, the train from Willow's wedding dress lay coiled up like a satin muff in her lap. She looked out the window, her eyes alert and focused on a dirty sky as she watched a lone crow fly no more than ten feet above the car, gliding in the slow wind. Willow had removed her veil and headpiece, letting her hair fall down past her shoulders. She opened the car window and inhaled the salty air, then exhaled out the window and said quietly:

"I do."

Nobody heard her.

Marjorie sat beside her, holding a tissue to her red nose, crying for what she believed were her sins of omission. Why had she not tried to get Willow to tell Graham the truth? Willow patted her hand, then turned towards the window again as one black crow feather spiralled through the air. Willow reached out the window and caught it as the crow flew away.

When Willow and her parents arrived home, she scrunched her gown into a paper shopping bag and set it on fire in the middle of a golden field. The eloquent bodice caught the first flame. The full skirt made a crying sound as the flames roared upwards. When the ashes cooled, she collected them in a tin can.

Willow returned to the house and saw that the icing on her wedding cake had begun to melt. "Men have no idea how wedding cakes weep," she said aloud as she kicked open the screen door to throw the cake to the crows.

Sometimes at night, she would read the note Graham mailed to her a few weeks after he left, tracing each word in the darkness with a small flashlight, searching for meaning under the stroke of her finger.

Dear Willow:

There is too much distance between us to catch up. I've met someone else. I wish you well. You are a strong woman. Follow your strength. It will take you a long way. I know what I did was cowardly. I should have told you before you were left to face such humiliation and hurt on your own. I am sorry and will always remember what we shared.

Graham

It read like an emotional prescription: an ounce of strength daily for Willow for the rest of her life. What did this coward know about what she needed? A face-to-face conversation before the wedding would have kept her out of the church. She carried Graham Currie's last words to her, shared on the altar the night before she was to become his wife: "I will always love you," he had said to her, before running from the church. Years later, when she let her flashlight find his words under her quilt, she would lash out. "Son of a bitch, how dare you remember what we shared. What we shared ran out of me like a river of red violence at my feet."

She'd saved a memento from every tragedy she'd ever experienced. As a child, she had refused to fly another kite after she lost her moon-and-stars to the wind, but she kept a strip of blue silk from that kite her mother had made. Days after the event, Rhona had found the silk remnant in Journey's End Cemetery, of all places for the wind to drop it off. Perhaps this was why Willow had stayed in Glenmor. She had planted little parcels of energy with Graham deep in the mountains where her fallen moon-and-stars kite had disappeared. Energy never dies. She buried the ashes of her wedding dress under a red maple and would later sit under the tree for hours, processing her anger and pain.

The morning after her abandoned wedding day, Willow walked to the Journey's End Cemetery and made a visit to Mary Ann's and John Duncan's graves. She wanted to be alone. Her parents and Marjorie watched as she walked away from the house.

She leaned against Mary Ann's tall tombstone and looked over towards John Duncan's stone. She and Graham had spent so much time here together during their school years. She had never seen anyone else visit Mary Ann's and John Duncan's graves in all the time she and Graham had spent here.

For the first time, Willow pondered the distance between the two graves, a green spread of only a few feet. Mary Ann's stone was tall grey marble, nearly ten feet high and shaped like a slim lighthouse. Her deeply carved name was barely visible now. Willow could read it from memory. *Here lies a woman in all her glory with nowhere to go* was written in Gaelic. Willow had had it translated. She smiled when she read what many people believed was a prayer. Whoever had this carved in stone knew Mary Ann very well. Graham believed that Mary Ann might have written her own epitaph.

John Duncan's inscription was modest and carved on a smaller marble stone: *Rest in the arms of Jesus*. Hopefully so, Willow thought to herself. There were many rumours in the community about the spinster and the bachelor who had died a week apart. Mary Ann died first, followed by John Duncan. They were both in their sixties. It was believed that poor John Duncan's heart sputtered out when he heard the news about the woman he had loved for years. Mary Ann had been found dead in her parlour chair wearing a satin dressing gown and a pair of silver high-heeled shoes. Was she expecting someone? No one would ever know. Perhaps this was when she had written her own message for all to see.

Willow felt at peace near these stones. Nobody was staring at her. Nobody was wondering how the millionaire's beautiful daughter could have taken such a fall. She wondered what Mary Ann would have thought of Willow's failed wedding day. Mary Ann might have laughed it off and told her to save the dress for another wedding.

"There are lots of fish in the sea, girl," Willow imagined Mary Ann saying, her voice defiant, rowdy and unleashed. "He'll be back with his tail between his legs. They all return when they grow allergic to the same sheets. History is not defined by loss, and neither is love. If so, the world would have come to an end because of a couple of loose fig leaves."

Willow left the cemetery and walked slowly along the path towards the church where she and Graham should have been married. She entered through the side door and was surprised to see vases of wildflowers placed along the floor on both sides of the altar. Her mother and Marjorie had decorated the church, but Willow had no memory of seeing the flowers the day before. Hanging from the pews, in the middle, were sprays of lavender mingled with Queen Anne's lace, tied with off-white bows from the leftover material from her wedding dress.

Willow sat in the back pew and laid her head against a pillar and closed her eyes. The church smelled like an open field. The scent of lavender was strong, lingering in the windless air. There was no sound except for the occasional groans in the old pine boards above her head. A lone ceiling fan buzzed like a queen bee as it slowed, shook and spun into silence.

Willow opened her eyes and watched a shadow move along the wall. She had not heard the door open. Turning, she saw a woman standing with her back against the wall.

"Hello," Willow said to the oldest face she had ever seen. Pale blue-grey eyes kept a steady glare on Willow. There was a trace of neither a frown nor a smile on her wrinkled brow. Waves of white hair fell to her shoulders. She was as tall as a child and dressed in a white frock.

"Can you speak English?" asked Willow.

The woman didn't answer.

Willow could hear men's voices coming from the vestry behind the altar. She turned from the woman and looked towards the front of the church. The voices faded away. "They must be looking for the old woman," Willow thought. She turned towards the woman, but she was gone. There had been no footsteps, no sound of a door being opened.

Willow ran to the door to the outside and opened it. There was no one in sight. She checked the back of the church. She went back outside and checked the vestry door. It was locked. Two men came around the corner. One was carrying a set of keys.

"Were you in the vestry a few minutes ago?" she asked.

"Yes, we were. Are you looking for someone?" the older man asked. "We'll be back later to take the decorations down."

"I was in the church. I saw an old woman behind me. I spoke to her, but she didn't answer me. She wasn't much bigger than a child. She just seemed to vanish."

The men looked at each other. "Miss, we haven't seen anyone around. There are lots of elderly folks in Glenmor, but they don't live close enough to the church to get here on their own."

"She was alone, the old lady I saw. She had long, wavy hair down to her shoulders." Willow's voice quivered.

"Do you live around here? We can give you a ride home," said one of the men. She could see a look of concern in their eyes.

"No, thank you. I don't need a ride."

"You don't look like the superstitious kind, miss, so I will tell you an old wives' tale my grandmother told us over and over again when we were kids."

His friend laughed. "I know that story myself."

"Whenever there was a wedding or a funeral in the parish, there was an old woman seen at the back of the church. Very few people ever saw her face to face. She only appeared to special people. They say she helped the deceased cross over into heaven."

The other man continued the story. "When she appeared at weddings, she put a special wish on the couple, especially the bride, whom she believed carried the most weight. Once the bride dropped the bouquet, her arms would be filled with children, according to the old woman."

Willow took a deep breath and thanked the two men for the story. She was embarrassed that she had even mentioned the sighting to the two strangers. Willow dismissed the old wives' tale, choosing instead to believe that she had fallen asleep when she leaned against the pillar for a few minutes. The old woman was just a dream. And yet there was something familiar in her grey-blue eyes.

The sky turned a darker colour, and a few drops of rain began to fall. Willow looked over her shoulder at the church as she walked away. She watched the red vigil candle flickering on the wall, its dizzy dance moves reflecting through a stained glass window.

She would not tell her mother about her visit to the church, or about the old woman. Her mother would believe the tale. "That was a forerunner, Willow," her mother would say. "She could see your future and wanted you to know that you will be happy again one day. There is another altar waiting for you."

===

CHAPTER THIRTEEN

Out of Words

WILLOW CAN HEAR A WOODPECKER IN A TREE above her father's workshop as she walks along the Alexander property towards the foot of the mountain. The summer is coming to an end. Graham is expected back any time now to take up practice at the clinic. So much has happened in Glenmor. Kathleen and James Millhouse's deaths have left the village in peril. A mixture of pity and anger fills the daily conversations around Glenmor. The local paper covered the story of the couple's deaths. The reporters stopped asking questions when they saw the look of grief on Willow Alexander's beautiful face.

As Willow walks around her property, she recalls a conversation she had with Dr. Millhouse about her father's health years earlier. She had been working at the clinic for a few months then. Willow knew her father's health was in decline shortly before her planned wedding day. Yet he'd refused to get any medical help.

"Family history," Dr. Millhouse declared to Willow when she finally asked for advice on her father's health. "There are no cures for genetics. There's an assembly of weak arteries in the Alexander family, I suspect. Send him in if he'll come. I've yet to meet a man who can count the steps he has left on this earth."

Willow listened intently but said nothing. She didn't like Dr. Millhouse or his prognosis. She wished she hadn't asked for his advice. Dr. Millhouse had arrived in 1964 from somewhere out west—Winnipeg, she believed. He came to Glenmor along with his ailing wife, Kathleen, to take over the old doctor's practice. Kathleen and Willow became great friends once Willow began working at the clinic after Graham left in 1970, after Willow had completed her medical secretary degree.

The sun was like a boil at the edge of a black cloud outside Dr. Millhouse's office window the day she asked about her father. The air was mouldy with dampness from the night rain. Outside, two small boys, carefree and healthy as cherubs, jumped into a mud puddle in their rubber boots.

Dr. Millhouse's voice cut in over the shrieking boys. "I'll have a word with him myself if you're not up to it." He waited for Willow to respond before he continued. "Your father is too practical for miracles and too intelligent to try to add an extension to the inevitable." He paused. "I'll give him something for the cough."

As Willow walked home from the doctor's office that day, she saw her father walking towards his workshop. His shoulders were hunched as he slowly made his way along the path. She had an urge to run to him, to inject her own strength into his weak arteries, a river of new life. She could see her mother in the kitchen window, watching him. She too must have seen Murdoch's slow steps. Rhona watched his every move these days. His smiles, partly interrupted by pain now, were faded. It was his eyes that completed his smiles when he looked at her or Willow. Rhona didn't seem to notice Willow walking towards the house from work.

Willow decided not to interrupt her father in his workshop. It was the only form of therapy he had left—wood and wisdom. The last thing that came off his lathe from his gifted hands was a set of maple canisters, a wedding gift for her and Graham. He smiled when he showed them to her and saw her face. It was an elegant domestic offering created to last a lifetime. She had carefully untied the gold ribbon and removed the sheet of gold wrapping paper, then buried the canisters in a trunk and closed the lid. It was the only wedding gift she had opened. The others she had returned.

Her mother didn't look up when Willow entered the kitchen. A pot of stew simmered in soft bubbles on the stove. "Your father's favourite," she said to Willow. Fresh bread in rows of golden crusts was lined up on the counter. Finally, her mother turned slowly to face Willow. "Would you make sure he gets a good bowl of stew in him for supper? And a glass of milk. I have an errand to take care of for an hour or so."

"You can't run away forever, Mother," Willow said. "You know his time is limited. Your errands will catch up with you." Willow's voice was cool and urgent, and as desperate as her mother's. "He likes it when you're here. I know he waits for you to return."

"I hate to see him struggle, especially when he eats. He's a proud man, Willow. Always was. You know that. He gets annoyed when he spills food on himself. I offer to help, but he won't let me. I don't believe your father was ever a child."

"The doctor gave me some medicine for his cough," Willow said, her voice softening.

Her mother turned her head to avert her eyes from another bottle of something or other. Everything in this house was connected to— She wasn't able to finish her thought. The house was dying along with her Murdoch. The walls, their clothes, their food, their words—everything held the aroma of the cold, damp vapour of death marinating the seams in the Alexander home.

Willow looked deeply into the eyes of the woman who loved her father as much as she did. She loved her mother for wanting to protect him. Their shared grief over Murdoch was already set. Willow remembered how she had melted into her father's shoulders as a child. He'd walk with her through the trees of the mountain, holding her high, pointing out the red maples, the white birch. Evergreen needles clung like barrettes to her hair.

Willow's mother escaped each evening into the mist for hours, returning when Murdoch was in bed for the night. He'd always called out her name when he heard the screen door open. And she would go as far as the bedroom door and whisper in to him, "Have a good night." She could not bear getting too close to what was left of her dying husband.

Willow watched as her mother walked towards the bend in the road, her hair, still a natural blond, pulled back into a French twist. Over her shoulders she had draped a green shawl. She didn't look like a housewife who had just made stew and baked bread. She looked too delicate a woman to be wilted by the heat of a late summer kitchen.

Later, her father returned to the bedroom from his workshop. From the downstairs bedroom, Murdoch listened to the small creaks of the burning spruce wood he had cut and packed into the woodbox. He had offered several times to buy an electric range for the pantry, but the idea met with his wife's disapproval.

"They burn everything to a crisp, Murdoch. A wood stove has even heat. I've seen the things that come out of those electric contraptions. You can't beat a wood stove. They are the heart of a kitchen."

The mantel clock on the old kitchen shelf struck four chimes. A lone blue jay guarded the discarded vegetable peelings outside, remnants of the simmering stew. Murdoch looked out at the peelings not far from his bedroom window. Three or four crows circled the feast. A blue-feathered dictator kept a steady eye on the advancing army. Soon, the jay's shrill cry bombed the still air, and black feathers waved in unison before fleeing into the trees.

Murdoch could see the slight figure of his wife beyond the fence. She stopped once or twice on her walk to adjust her shawl. Rhona looked lovely. She always did. He could see the contour of her body being enveloped by the mist, wisps of green disappearing like leaves under soft snow. He wanted to get up and go to her, wrap his arms around the shawl for extra warmth, whisper, "I love you." For the first time in months, he realized how much he loved and missed her. They'd met decades ago at a dance. In that era, dances were responsible for most of the marriages in Glenmor, the music waltzing people together.

"Murdoch," she'd said as a young bride, "you never say 'I love you' out loud."

"Out loud is overrated, Rhona," he replied. "Pay attention to what a man does, not what he says."

"What about when we make love?"

"Making love doesn't require a language."

"Okay," she replied softly. "I believe you."

He shuddered now at the lame excuses he'd given to such

a good woman. Many times she'd offered him money from her inheritance for something new—a truck, a saw, lumber. How strong he'd felt at politely refusing her offerings.

She'd always nod her head in response, and say softly, "If you need anything, just ask. The bank isn't far away."

How proud he'd been not to take his wife's money. Her Cropper inheritance was never really discussed in the family. And even now, he was still refusing her help. How often had she offered to help him eat his food? And he refused. He was so unlike his own father, who would have eaten out of his mother's hand. Murdoch didn't possess his father's amorous chords, though. Murdoch loved Rhona in a quiet way. What thrilled him most was the dampness of her skin, as though he were making love to a woman who had just walked out from under a waterfall and fallen upon his bed.

Willow interrupted his thoughts, a bowl of stew teetering on a tray. "Mother asked me to bring this in to you."

"I'm not really hungry, child." He had not called her "child" for years.

Willow was in a talking mood. She knew her father's words were running out. "Did I ever tell you why I would never fly another kite?"

Murdoch turned to face his daughter and listened to her voice.

"I didn't want to disappoint you and Mother. I didn't want you to feel like you failed, but I was wrong. You never did fail me in any way."

"Take care of your mother, Willow, and you will never fail yourself. She will need you beside her. And I know you can do whatever it takes, my girl."

Willow turned her head towards the window. She always avoided emotional discussions with her father. She also disliked watching his chest heave as he took a deep breath, his conversations laboured.

"Do me a favour, Willow. Put the stew back in the pot until your mother gets home. I'll eat it then!"

Willow looked down at her father. His breathing was calmer now—too calm. There was a whisper to his voice, like a child secretly bargaining with Santa Claus for something special. Her mother entered the room behind her. Willow hadn't heard her come in.

"The fog's rolling in like silent thunder. I had to turn back," her mother said.

Willow passed her mother the tray and left the room.

Her mother understood.

Rhona's hand trembled as she dipped the spoon into the stew to feed her husband. As Murdoch watched her, he imagined he was seeing her for the first and last time. His mouth opened painfully for the offering. The food went down slowly. Another half spoonful. Then two more.

"You're doing well, Murdoch," Rhona assured him with a smile.

One more spoonful caused a slight dribble down his chin, and she caught it with the napkin. Murdoch reached up and touched her hand that held the spoon. The spoon fell to the floor. A blue-and-white streak crossed the window. The bird turned and landed on the ledge. The window was slightly open, allowing the bird to witness the last moments of a husband and wife who had run out of words. Rhona began to weep as the red bowl of stew crashed to the floor.

The blue jay watched silently as Murdoch Alexander drew his last breath.

‡ ‡ ‡

MURDOCH'S TWO BROTHERS were out west and returned on occasion. His sisters were matrimonially scattered throughout the province. Occasionally they would visit their brother in the summer months, and they would sit around recalling old events that they carried with them, memories that kept the family united. The siblings' last visit with their brother had been earlier that summer, before Dr. Millhouse's prognosis. Recalling the visit was a seesaw of memories for Willow. His sisters saw the dark moons rising under his eyes, his lean frame on a slant. He had not rolled up the sleeves of his plaid shirt as usual, keeping his thin arms under wraps, which swayed like off-stroke oars whenever he raised them.

Murdoch's oldest sister, Cassie, was the family storyteller. "Remember, Murdoch, when the crazy aunts appeared like unexpected summer storms to check up on us? How you kept your cool when they burned the catalogues from the outhouse and introduced us to toilet paper!" Murdoch and his sisters broke into hysterics. "The way you liked to read everything, Murdoch, I was sure you'd throw them out on their ear."

Margaret, the youngest sister, piped in, "I was the lucky one when you drew my name to be maid of honour at your wedding." She chuckled. "You felt putting our names in a bag and making a draw was the only fair way to decide."

"It was rigged," the other two said, laughing. "You were always the favourite."

Margaret had the deep, dark contours of their mother Bella's beautiful face, which was childlike in its oval presentation. Margaret had large, dark eyes that found beauty in misshapen trees and turbulent tides. She spoke the language of the birds of the sky and the animals of the forest, and could have lived her life in the lost paradise of nature. Murdoch was grateful she'd married a botanist who recognized her ethereal qualities and fathered two children with her. They travelled to exotic countries every year, where she always sought to feed the birds and the animals from an open hand.

Willow had observed her father's siblings from the stuffed chair in the parlour. She tried to imagine what it would be like if the two Cropper sisters had come for a visit. Sitting side by side like omens, drinking tea. Smoking Cuban cigars

and speaking Spanish as they inhaled a Glenmor gather-
ing. Her mother would have gone out of her way to enter-
tain them. But with Murdoch's sisters, Willow just flitted
between them, dropping tidbits about their life in Glenmor.

"Your brother has a way with women," Rhona had
said to his sisters. They applauded in unison, waiting for
a punchline that Rhona did not deliver. Instead, she began
to cough up remnants of a dry biscuit and forgot what she
was about to say. Murdoch held his quiet smile under his
right hand.

The collection of misty-eyed female siblings surrounding Murdoch began discussing their mother's sudden death.
They recalled their father's arm on their mother's shoulder when he'd return from the woods, his fingers delicately
spread, the way he kneaded the tired trouble spots of his
beloved wife, Bella, in moments of domestic intimacy. The
light and dark trials of their childhoods were alive with the
memories of their ghosts. Their mother had sudden out-
bursts after their father's death. "Widow's nerves" it was
called. After weeks of silence, there would suddenly be too
much noise, and it was nerve-racking. They would make
midnight visits to the cemetery with their mother, Murdoch
ahead with the lantern as Bella trailed in the path of moving light towards the grave. They would watch Bella's arms
rise and fall as she knelt beside her husband's resting place,
delivering a silent monologue before weeping openly. The
day after the grave visits, she would sleep until noon.

"Why didn't you wake me, Murdoch? You know how much there is to do around here," she'd scold.

"You needed the rest, Mama."

"You need meals."

"Our neighbour brought over a pot of soup and fresh bread."

"That's *my* job, Murdoch. Your father loved my soup."

Murdoch was twenty-four when his mother passed away. A full moon kept company with the lovely Bella Alexander until dawn. Her face as still as glass. She had let her hair down and it fanned a halo around her head. A slight smile sealed her lips. The rising sun lit up her beauty in bouquet patterns. Her hands spread evenly along the patchwork quilt she'd made for her marriage bed. She had taken to her bed a week before, giving orders for nothing but strong black tea. The Alexander clan then gathered for one more funeral. A collection of Alexanders arrived from universities around the country. They circled the mound of clay that would blanket their beautiful mother next to their father. The wind was edgy that day, scattering dust and sprinkling the family wreath like cinnamon.

Murdoch's siblings left three days after Bella's funeral. Murdoch stood in the middle of the road for a while after they drove away. He was in no hurry to do anything. He had a house and land and silence rolling down off the mountain to keep him company.

‡ ‡ ‡

IT IS HARD to read a man of few words, yet Willow often dove in, questioning her father about his life. Why didn't he go to university after his mother died? He was still very young.

"There was nothing stopping you," Willow said. "You made sure that all your siblings were educated."

He smiled up at his only child. This was a fair question, he supposed. Time or circumstances had not stopped him from doing anything.

"I considered it a few times, Willow. Then unconsidered it. What would I do with an engineering degree in Glenmor?"

"Move out of Glenmor," she answered. "You would have left if your father hadn't died so young."

Murdoch rubbed his chin. "I had two choices: go back to school or stay in the mountains. When a man reaches a certain level of contentment, he's already reached his goals." He smiled.

"Well," said Willow, "I still believe you were robbed."

"I was robbed of nothing but a few sleepless nights, child. I spent the time studying engineering courses that came in the mail. I even have a diploma that fits snugly in the bottom of my old trunk."

"An engineering diploma? Why didn't you tell anyone?"

"I just did. Now you know. I'm a paper engineer." He cast a side glance towards his daughter. "Why is it necessary that anyone should know?"

Years later, after Murdoch's own health declined, Willow watched her mother flitting around the room, offering more tea and oatcakes to his sisters on their final visit. Murdoch had never raised his voice. He had what all wise men seek: silent strength. Willow had never once heard her parents quarrel. They slept in separate rooms for a few years, which her mother said was her idea. Her mother was a painter, and felt the draw of the brush was a spiritual stroke that could be sent to her at any moment. The idea of disturbing her husband at any hour of darkness led her to her solo dreams. Besides, Murdoch needed undisturbed rest; he awoke at five every morning to begin his day. Willow knew very little at the time about the courtship of her parents, or the chemistry that led them to a field of wet daisies for an out-of-focus photo after their wedding vows.

Murdoch nodded his head slowly as his sisters talked. Then he felt a quick slice of pain to his chest. He slipped a pill under his tongue with sleight of hand. His mortality calendar flipped its pages frequently. But Murdoch Alexander wasted none of his time on regret.

Murdoch and Rhona walked the Alexander sisters to their car at the end of their last summer visit. Willow had watched from the verandah steps. She caught the nervous chatter coming through the half-circle the women had formed around their brother, words drowning and fighting for air. The sinking sun made them look baked in their white skin. The two with carrot tops looked bronzed. Margaret, the youngest, curled her arms around her brother. The maid of honour, picked from a bag, had special privileges.

They waved offhandedly at Willow as though they were shooing away mosquitoes. She had never been a friendly child around them, or even as a young adult. She roamed through their conversations like a mime. Rhona, although as nervous as a hen under an axe, was very friendly and was always liked by everyone. And dear Murdoch, quiet and wise. Loved forever.

‡ ‡ ‡

RHONA WAITED FOR weeks after her husband's passing to clear out his belongings. A Salvation Army pickup truck backed up to the door, loaded Murdoch's humble ward-robe, then rode off down the mountain road. Rhona kept his raincoat and rubber boots for emergencies. She stood at the open gate long after the truck was out of sight. Summer had dropped enough rain into her flower gardens to pro-duce a vibrant burst of colour along the picket fence. The sunflowers whispered and bowed their heads towards the frail woman standing in the open gateway.

Murdoch's "sickroom" became Rhona's bedroom after the clearing. She had no more desire to climb the stairs every night. Climbing steep stairs caused her headaches and dizziness, she announced. She preferred to be closer to the ground, she said when Willow asked about the change in her sleeping arrangements.

"We don't live in the Empire State Building, Mother. You have strong walking legs. You can walk forever," Willow replied. Her mother had never complained about headaches or dizziness before. More than likely it was stress, Willow decided as she set up the downstairs bedroom for her mother.

Rhona said she planned to work on a new painting once she got settled. On the easel at the foot of her bed rested a blank canvas awaiting the first stroke. She never let Willow know ahead of time what she had waiting at the tip of her brush.

"Why didn't you both move into your big house when you married?" Willow asked out of curiosity as she arranged the room for her.

"A man wouldn't think of letting a woman put a roof over his head, dear, especially your father when he had his own home to offer me," Rhona replied. "I would have lived with your father in a tree house, Willow. A woman will take anything when she's in love."

Willow smiled at her mother's sentimentality, as she watched her nod off to sleep.

CHAPTER FOURTEEN

Nightly Vigil

WILLOW WOULD NOT GO TO THE CEMETERY TO visit her father's grave, even though her mother repeatedly requested it.

"I find comfort at his grave, Willow," Rhona said. "I'm sure you would too if you bothered to come along. Your father knows I'm there. I can tell."

"I'm not a dust worshipper, Mother. I would find no comfort near a mound of clay. You are much better at these things than I am. I wish I had your courage. You're much better with emotions than I am. You're a nicer person than I am." Willow hugged her mother as she prepared to set off for the cemetery. "One of these days I will go with you, Mother. But the last three years have been a blur."

"Where did that young fellow go, who was here with you all the time? You always liked to go up the mountain with him to pick berries. And where is that cute little girl? You were like sisters. You were always so much taller than her."

"He's working away now, Mother. He'll be back soon. And Marjorie lives away. She'll be home to stay one of these days."

This lapse in her mother's memory surprised Willow. She watched Rhona wrap a scarf around her head and close the screen door quietly behind her. She noticed her mother's thin shoulders turn slightly, her head at a left angle. Perhaps she was watching over her shoulder for the shadow of her daughter to appear, listening for the sound of scattered gravel as Willow shuffled to meet up with her. Willow watched from the pantry window and noticed the weight that had begun to peel from Rhona's slight frame. She could see the shuffle of grief as her mother walked along the road, oblivious as to what direction she was going to take.

Willow returned to the parlour, grabbed a book and sank into the chair. She turned to Henry, the wooden butler, to get a frontal view. She hadn't noticed the small painting on the ashtray before. The oil paint was still fresh. She avoided touching it. A small garden bloomed where the butts had once gathered, a mixture of colourful wildflowers, daisies, buttercups and dandelions taking a bow. Henry looked like a flower girl in a tuxedo. There was something whimsical in the painting. Henry stood at attention with his wet garden held carefully in his wooden hands. He had never failed them. He carried whatever was put in his hands with great panache.

Unlike her parents, Willow did not have a creative flair. She didn't sew or paint. Her mother and father were cheated of an artistic prodigy.

A sudden barrel roll of thunder above her head alarmed Willow. Branches of lightning scratched the sky. Rain began falling as hard as gravel. Willow looked out the parlour window; Rhona was nowhere in sight along the road. Her mother was still at the cemetery. Willow pulled her father's raincoat from the hook in the porch along with her own and made her way to the car. The rain was falling hard on the windshield. When Willow arrived at the entrance to the cemetery, she grabbed her father's raincoat off the seat. She found her mother's slim figure kneeling beside a muddy mound of clay, oblivious to the raging late summer storm. She resembled a statue, her hands cuffed in prayer and her feet as bare as a newborn's.

Willow threw the raincoat over her mother's shoulders and wrapped it around her slight body. "You have to get out of this storm, Mother! It's getting stronger by the minute."

Her mother remained silent. She felt like a doll in Willow's strong arms. Her body remained limp until they reached the house, where Willow drew her a warm bath.

"I was about to leave when the rain started. I couldn't see one foot in front of the other. I took my shoes off. They were covered in mud. It wasn't raining when I left home, then it was suddenly like a blizzard. You must think I'm mad. I thought it would stop as quickly as it started, so I just knelt there and waited. I was trapped in a storm with my dead husband six feet below. I saw someone walking along the graveyard path. I couldn't tell who the man was from where I was kneeling, but I know he noticed me. He stopped and looked my way. For some strange reason, I wasn't afraid. There was something familiar about him. He looked like your father. And you know that I've always believed in ghosts. They will return when you're in need of their help. And then, after I saw him, you came along, Willow. They know when you need help."

Willow swore under her breath but didn't respond. Perhaps, in her anxiety and panic, her mother had mistaken swaying branches for limbs or a tall stone for the lone figure of a man. She wondered if she should get Dr. Millhouse to prescribe something. Willow had noticed changes in her mother's mental state shortly after her father died, but she had passed it off as grief. Now she was beginning to worry.

"I knew this day would come, but that doesn't make it any easier. Your father spoke of death as if it were a road map through a sunny terrain that led to a paradise full of who knows what . . ." Tears streamed down her mother's face as she spoke.

Willow bit her lip.

"What do you suppose he meant, Willow?"

"I don't know. He could have meant rabbits or snap-dragons. He liked to joke with us. Remember that, Mother? How much he liked to make us laugh and we always did to please him? You must remember those times. There were plenty of times when we laughed together."

"Are you angry at me, Willow?"

"No, I'm angry at him for dying. I warned him about smoking."

There. Willow had said what she felt. How many times had she warned her father about smoking? There was no reason to get into anything with her mother when she was so fragile from her loss. She knew there was no way her mother would have asked him to quit smoking. Willow always believed his smoking was the real reason her mother had moved to her own room. She never believed her mother's story about not wanting to disturb her father's rest when she felt like painting in the middle of the night. They were cross-the-hall lovers. It had been rather amusing to Willow at the time.

Willow put her mother into bed and held a cup of tea in her hand, letting her sip the hot brew. Her mother muttered on until she fell asleep, talking about a tombstone. Willow pulled the blanket under her chin and left the room quietly.

The sky was breaking into patches like a picture puzzle when Willow returned to the parlour. She picked *Crime and Punishment* off the floor where it had fallen and placed it on the table. The book wasn't nearly as intriguing as her mother's graveyard story. She pulled her feet into the chair and curled up like a cat. But she couldn't read. The words blurred in front of her. The house was as silent as an empty church. The rain had stopped. Willow kept an ear open for her mother's voice.

Her mind wandered back to the graveyard. Did her mother really see someone there? A man. Maybe it was Graham, Willow thought. Was it possible that he might have sneaked home for a visit? Willow had no idea why such a ludicrous idea would pop into her head like that. But she couldn't let it go. What would he be doing in the graveyard? As far as she knew, no one in his family had died recently. Besides, he would have taken his wife with him. She was a tall brunette with bangs that covered most of her eyebrows, a doctor who specialized in the corrosion of bones. Maybe Graham had thought it was Willow in the graveyard and didn't have the nerve to approach her.

Willow stopped. A slant to her face, the beginning of a smile, melted like a snowball dropped into hot water. Willow threw *Crime and Punishment* across the room. Why could this man still cause such a storm in her life?

—

CHAPTER FIFTEEN

Beauty and Blood

WILLOW PICKED UP HER BOOK, LAID IT BACK ON the table and then crept upstairs so she wouldn't wake her mother. In her dream that night, Graham appeared. He was a groom, dressed in the suit he probably would have worn to their wedding. He was running down the aisle of the church, looking for someone. The church was empty, but a Gregorian chant drifted from the choir loft above his head. He burst out of the church, then jumped over the stair railings to the ground. Someone with a wise face—she realized clearly now, it was her father—tried to help him up, but Graham wrestled himself free and kept running towards the mountain and disappeared into the woods.

The dream ended abruptly when Willow was awakened by her mother calling out for another pair of socks. Willow walked down the stairs to her mother's bedroom and found her sitting up in bed with a woollen sweater over her night-dress. She looked shyly towards her daughter, afraid that, as a grown woman calling for help in the middle of the night, she'd turned into the child.

"My bones are ice, Willow, and my feet have caught the chill."

Willow noticed red blotches creeping up along her mother's face. She felt her mother's forehead, which fired off heat into Willow's hand.

"You have a fever, Mother. I'll get you a couple of Aspirins."

"Did I catch this fever in the graveyard? Your father would think I was silly for being there in a storm."

"I don't think so. The dead don't have fevers. You've been visiting his grave for more than three years now, ever since he passed on. You were probably coming down with something before you got caught in the storm. I'll have Dr. Millhouse stop by and check you out tomorrow after work."

"I had a dream about the man in the graveyard," Rhona said. "I know I've seen him before. He called out my name as if he knew me from long ago." Her words came with intervals of short pauses.

Willow sat beside the bed and sang to her the Gaelic song she'd sung since she was a child, until her mother fell back to sleep. She went into the kitchen and made a small fire in the stove. She opened the parlour windows to get a breath of fresh air. Slow drops of rain licked the window-panes clean. Her mother always closed the downstairs windows at night; she worried a fox might get in through the screens. It was Thursday, and Willow had a half-day's work ahead of her in the morning. She wondered, as she put on the kettle for tea, if perhaps Dr. Millhouse could come to the house in the afternoon.

In the parlour, Willow pulled Henry closer to her. The painting on the ashtray was dry now. Henry had a new lease on life. There would be no more ashes or butts to destroy his garden.

"You are smoke-free," Willow said to Henry's profile. He looked as though he were listening intently to something. In the kitchen, the kettle began to hum, slowly then loudly, filling the kitchen with a mystical drone.

Later that morning, Dr. Millhouse listened to Willow, sensing perhaps that she was downplaying her mother's illness, her voice flat-toned and emotionless but her description exact and without alarm.

"I'll drop by after four. Your father's passing has been hard on her these last few years."

"I'm aware of that," Willow said.

"How was she when you left for work?"

"Listless, but her fever was down."

After work that afternoon, Willow left the office and gritted her teeth as she made her way home. The idea of having to ask Dr. Millhouse to come to the house annoyed her. He had a fatal, scientific intellect. Whatever he diag-nosed came true. He reminded Willow of a fortune teller—an oracle with an unruly beard and moustache who spit out life and death in the same sentence.

She took a deep breath and walked slowly. Behind her, the tides were reversing, the sea moaning in its depths as if drowning into itself. Next to her, five children were play-ing in an open field, stomping on empty milk cans that gripped around the edge of their shoes as they broke into a graceful gallop. Silver hoofs, light and daring on their feet. Two of the girls in the pack began to nuzzle each other like playful ponies. They'd let down their blond ponytails. Manes of yellow hair covered their faces. The boys began to race one another, neighing at the starting line. Willow watched until they were down the hill out of sight. She had an urgent desire to go to the top of the hill to watch what played out next. Which spirited young colt had won the race? She could hear their cheerful voices rising up from below. As a young child she had thought of this game as childish fantasy, a waste of time when she'd prefer to read a book. She was never picked for games with other kids. She and Marjorie made up their own games. Graham liked ball games and hockey with the boys.

"Let her read her friggin' books," the kids would say with scowls, and she always pretended she didn't hear them. Had she wasted her childhood on reality? At this stage in her life, she wished she could trot along the road wearing tin cans and scatter the gravel in her path, let her hair down and examine the texture of green grass close to the ground. Had her own child lived to see the light of day—had she not miscarried a month after Graham left her at the altar—who knew? Perhaps her child would have been playing with these children on this day instead of being rooted under a maple tree on the mountain. Willow pulled her scarf tightly around her head to ease the migraine she felt coming on.

When Willow arrived home, her mother called out to her just as she closed the door behind her.

Her mother was munching on something when Willow walked into the room. "I've been eating dry crackers all morning. This is all I could eat in the morning for weeks when I was expecting you, Willow. Do you suppose this is why you hate crackers?"

"Are you expecting now, Mother?" Willow gently teased. "How are you feeling now? I'm home with you for the night. I can read a story to you if you wish. I know you love to listen to stories being read to you."

"I'm feeling a little better. I feel a bit chilled. Do you suppose I could be in the family way? I always wanted children."

"The doctor will be over around four to check you out." Willow smiled as she hugged her mother. "I always wanted children too, Mother."

Rhona changed the subject. "Why did you have to bother the doctor? That poor wife of his needs him more than I do. She hides in a closet all day, you know. Nobody sees her about."

"I see her every day, Mother. She's quite beautiful. And she's a nice lady to talk to. I bring her baked goods. She loves chocolate cake."

"Maybe he'll be angry that you bothered him, Willow."

"He won't be bothered. He's addicted to illness." Willow shook her head and grinned.

"The poor man is so bedraggled-looking. I hope his wife's illness is not contagious. It's a blessing they don't have children."

"No, it's not contagious, Mother. I bring her tea at lunchtime every day."

"You should offer him a bit of supper, Willow. He looks like he lives out of a can. Perhaps he would like a glass of lemonade—I made a jug today. Or give him a drink of rum. That will coax his appetite into high gear. I like moonshine myself."

Willow chuckled to herself at the thought of her mother drinking moonshine. Her mother's lips had never been dampened by liquor. Willow tucked away these non-sensical conversations with her mother to ease what she knew would soon be another loss.

Willow smirked at the thought of Dr. Millhouse trotting down the road with cans on his feet. She recalled Irene, his housekeeper, who was a good cook, and cleaned the place to a shine. One morning, after the doctor had left the office on a call, Irene came over to speak to Willow.

"I've seen more meat on a scarecrow," she had said. "But he eats like a horse." She wiped her brow. "Strangest man I ever met, except for my uncle Rory. He hung wine bottles on the branches of a tree. He believed he could grow wine with this invention."

Willow decided not to offer supper to Dr. Millhouse. The thought of his moustache dipping into a china cup of tea soured her appetite. She made tea for him at noon every day, placing the pot on his desk with a deep mug. He always devoured the homemade sweets she brought to him.

Dr. Millhouse arrived at exactly 4 p.m. He walked in with his laces untied and his glasses hanging on a slant. There were buttons missing from his cardigan. He smelled of iodine. Willow retreated to the parlour when he went in to check her mother. Henry stood with his flower ashtray, as firm as a stone lion, facing the middle of the room. He was placed directly where he used to stand for the card games, to collect the long-ago ashes and butts of her father and his friends. Had her mother been in the parlour and moved things about? Willow had not moved Henry.

She could hear a scramble of words between her mother and Dr. Millhouse coming down the hall and through the parlour door, Rhona's voice childlike, a mouthful of merriment from a distance, the doctor's always even and low-keyed.

Willow then heard the doctor shuffling his way down the hall towards her. As she put her book back on the side table, she looked up to find him in the doorway, with his untied laces, his buttonless cardigan, his hidden smile and his smell of iodine. He refused a chair.

"Your mother is not well, and it's not the cognitive cloud of grief that frequents the mind of the bereaved. She has, I suspect, a tumour of the brain that could end her life quite suddenly. But I will have her tested to be sure. I'm going to Sydney on Monday. I'll take her with me, if you can stay with Mrs. Millhouse until I return. I'll stay with her and take her for the test myself." His tone was flat, observant and complete.

Willow breathed deeply, like a professional smoker, then exhaled towards him. "She's never complained of headaches," she blurted out as if to contradict his prognosis. But she was not being truthful. She did remember her mother complaining of headaches and dizziness. It was the reason she'd given for moving to the downstairs bedroom.

"There are no telltale signs to the naked eye in the early stages of this form of cancer," he said without emotion. "She may not be able to identify any symptoms. But if it's what I think it is, she will eventually lose her vision. And she will suffer from cognitive interference and will not be able to repair a broken sentence towards the end.

But that's only if she does have a tumour, but I believe that she does."

Willow's eyes focused on the doctor who had delivered news of impending death not once but twice in a matter of a few years. She wanted him to leave, to take his rumpled self and disappear. But he continued to speak.

"I suggest, Willow, that you have someone stay with her while you are not home for any period of time. She will become very absent-minded. I will call a colleague of mine in Sydney and have her admitted to hospital when I can no longer do anything more for her at home. It will be impossible for you to take care of your mother when the condition worsens."

And then he was gone, his visit leaving behind the fetid smell of iodine in the house for days. Willow sat back in her chair before she went in to see her mother. The air was still. She could hear no sounds either inside or outside the house. She felt suspended in time, an orphan of the inevitable, where neither time nor sound could penetrate. It was not quite four years since her father had passed away. Had her mother been ill back then, she wondered.

Her mother was cheerful when Willow looked in on her. She didn't mention Dr. Millhouse's visit. Instead, she asked if Willow's father was still up on the mountain.

"He works too hard, Willow. He could die on that mountain and still be a happy man."

Willow didn't reply, but instead left the room and made

a quick visit to her neighbour. She spoke in short senten-
ces, explaining the situation with her mother's health. Mrs.
Welsh arrived the next morning at 8 a.m. and stayed until
Willow returned home after work to a hot cooked meal.
From that point on, Willow paid Mrs. Welsh two hundred
dollars a week from the Cropper inheritance money. Shortly
after she began helping Willow, a new antenna appeared on
Mrs. Welsh's roof, and she began looking out at the land
from new windows. A new porch door greeted visitors.
Mrs. Welsh exploded with the release of poverty, elimin-
ated from her life due to whatever was growing in Rhona
Alexander's head.

Mrs. Welsh treated Rhona as lovingly as a child. She
made gingerbread men and cookies and let Rhona decor-
ate them. She crocheted a blanket to keep Rhona warm
when it rained. She answered Rhona gently when she called
her Mama, and pretended Rhona's mother was at her side.
Confused people didn't alarm Mrs. Welsh, and she asked
to sleep in the cot Willow set up in her mother's bedroom.

"You need your rest," she told Willow. "You have a full
working day ahead of you. I'm at home here with your
mother. She's no bother to me."

Dr. Millhouse made weekly visits to check in on Rhona.
She underwent the tests he ordered, which showed that
there was, in fact, a tumour, but it was growing slowly. The
doctor left strong pain medication with Willow for what
was to come. But before the pain struck, before her eyes

would catch their last sunset, Rhona painted. A blue jay appeared on the small canvas at the end of her bed. It stood behind a pane of glass, green-and-grey feathers sparse and clinging to a child's stick-like image of a bird. It had no wings but did have a smile under its beak.

"Do you remember this blue jay, Willow? He appeared at the window when your daddy died."

"Yes, Mother, I remember him." Willow smiled at her mother's painting. There was something whimsical about the bird's green colouring and wingless body. Despite its strange colour, the bird looked happy.

"Your father loved blue jays. He believed they were clever strategists. What day did he die, Willow? I believe you were out playing in the mist while I tried to feed him stew."

"It was a Friday, Mother. It was very foggy."

She watched the smile on her mother's face explode into laughter. "A heavy mist came down the day we were married. After the reception and dance, Murdoch carried me into the house and up the stairs. He said he had to, or he would lose me to the night." She gave a deep sigh that stopped the laughter. "We slid right into marriage. I barely had time to undress. He mentioned something about a waterfall. Oh, he had a way with women, that man. The next morning the sun fell upon our bed and found us as naked as blue jays."

Willow imagined her mother and father on their wedding night, a damp mass of red hair tangled with blond waves, their voices hushed for no reason other than to hear each other's whispers. They'd considered themselves blessed to have waited. Waiting would have been part of the ecstasy for her mother. She had probably even held a magic wand against the ghost of sex—temptation. Finally, she had defeated the ghost and could reach for her husband. Willow thought her mother had remained naive enough to believe that he had never touched another woman, had never taken the scent of a Saturday night home and dropped it on his pillow. Many women loved him and wanted to marry him. And in lonely, cold marriage beds, on the wedding night of Rhona and Murdoch Alexander, only a few miles away, many sleepless women choked back his name.

CHAPTER SIXTEEN

===

Invisible Scribbles

OCTOBER 1979. SUNDAY AFTERNOON. A BURNT-orange flame of leaves covered Christy's Mountain. Strangers with cameras and tripods stood at the edge of the Alexander property, hanging their camera cases on the fence posts. They were there to behold the beauty of the mountain, to frame her in all her glory. The mountain was, as always, seductive and willing, sassy and proud. She waved and swayed, exposing what was left of her summer greens when she bowed.

Rhona sat at her bedroom window, her vision limited. She could see light shining through, but not much else. Rhona ran her small fingers along the windowpane, like a child, as Willow watched. Then she erased her drawing with the sleeve of her housecoat and began again. More mumbles and strokes, before a smile of satisfaction warmed her face.

"This is lovely," she exclaimed of the invisible scribbles on the windowpane. "I must paint this more often."

"What did you paint, Mother?"

"It's a tombstone, Willow. Can't you see it?"

"Yes, it's beautiful, Mother. I like it," Willow replied in a quiet voice. She didn't want her mother to hear the pain in it.

Willow put her mother back to bed before calling Mrs. Welsh to stay with her for the afternoon. Willow made her way along the road towards the cemetery before a feeling stalled her, a hammering in her chest. "A good place for a heart attack," she thought. "Why can't you just weep like normal people?"

Her heart still carried the first wound it picked up in this graveyard. She took a few slow steps towards the gate, waiting for silence in her chest. She hadn't been here since she'd carried her mother home in the storm. She moved slowly towards her father's grave, which was covered in fading green grass. A handful of orange leaves banked against the marble stone. The headstone was shaped like an open book. On the left, her father's name, Murdoch William Alexander; to the right, her mother's, Rhona Elizabeth Cropper Alexander. In the opening, between the pages, rested a gold leaf like a bookmark.

Rhona would have forgotten the headstone by now, but it didn't matter. She never did mention it. Her mother would rest here shortly. Waiting for Rhona, three rows down, Willow's grandparents, Jacob and Bella Alexander, lay at rest, their simple stones dulled but firm, their names unscarred by death as by life. An autumn garden of leaves was gathered between their stones, and a small mouse rummaged in and out of the pile, running for its life at the crunch of footsteps. Willow walked back to her father's resting place.

Willow checked the spot beyond the grave where her mother claimed to have seen the man standing and looking towards her. He would've been close enough to have called out her name. She spotted a tree nearby with broken limbs. An old tombstone on a slant near the spot caught Willow's eye. The name was eroded from the stone, leaving only three letters visible to the naked eye: *p*, *r* and *t*. Whoever rested beneath the stone had been erased by the winds of time.

Willow walked towards the graves of Mary Ann Mac-Iver and John Duncan MacSween. A bouquet of fresh flowers lay upon Mary Ann's grave, petunias in vibrant colours of red, mauve and yellow tied in a single strand of lace. They had been placed directly in the middle of the grave. Willow had never seen anyone at her grave before. She made a quick search of the bouquet for a card, but there was none. She would never know who left the last of summer's beauty here for Mary Ann.

Willow would have told her mother about the mysterious bouquet if Rhona had been capable of remembering.

Willow had heard her mother's theory about the spinster Mary Ann's grave next to the bachelor John Duncan's.

"The dear souls were probably in love in their youth but for some reason never married. Some kind soul made sure they were buried side by side. Willow, you know that destiny may not always be wise, but it is exact."

Willow recalled leaning on Mary Ann's tombstone when she'd said yes to Graham Currie's proposal of marriage. Mary Ann knew destiny well. She believed her script had already been written. Would this be Willow's tale to tell as well?

‡ ‡ ‡

AFTER LEAVING THE cemetery, Willow returned to the mountain, where a few strangers were still milling around. A rather large man pointed upwards towards the fiery trees. An eagle had him shifting from one foot to the other, like a clumsy youth learning to dance. A woman at his sleeve said something to him, but he continued to point upwards. The woman noticed Willow approaching along the fence. The man turned as Willow drew near. They were younger than they looked from a distance.

"Mighty mountain you have here," the man said.

Willow nodded in response. They told her they were from Texas. "On our honeymoon," they declared in unison.

"Getting a look at the east coast of Canada for the first time," the woman added.

Willow told them her name and left them with a few bits of history before she said goodbye and moved on. The man spoke once again. His voice, with a honeymoon glaze, was spiked with a quiet seduction. He wasn't the first man she'd met who was turned on by a mountain. He passed Willow his card.

"If you ever decide to sell your property, ma'am, we'd appreciate a call."

Willow took the card and walked slowly towards the gate, reducing the card to a fistful of confetti that she threw into the air.

No strangers would ever live under her father's roof as long as she was alive.

‡ ‡ ‡

THE FOLLOWING DAY, Willow said to Mrs. Welsh, "When I was at the cemetery yesterday, I noticed a fresh bouquet of flowers on Mary Ann MacIver's grave."

"Bless me twice, girl. If that woman were alive, she'd be nearing two hundred. Probably had a dinosaur for a pet when she was a child. They say she was the prettiest girl this side of the mountain. A teacher."

Willow's curiosity was kindled. "Why didn't she ever marry?"

"She loved the attention of more than one man. A wandering eye, they claim, is not looking for a husband—it's just looking. I don't believe there are any relatives left, except a few scattered here and there in the old graveyard. Yet others say her mother was taken advantage of by a married man and cast from her family like a rogue dog. When Mary Ann was born, she was left in an orphanage and never taken in by anyone, probably because of the curse that was stamped on her mother's loose offerings to a married man. Those things happened, you know. Women got blamed for things like that when their only crime was a beautiful face. Some say John Duncan's family put their foot down on his interest in her too. They believed Mary Ann was low and John Duncan's family was high in standards. Others believed it was Mary Ann who did the stomping; she loved him but would not cause any shame to him or his family. She knew what it was like to be not wanted from the cradle. She carried her own sorrow in the seams of her heart to the grave, if that was the case. The poor woman may have sacrificed her own happiness for his."

Willow questioned Mrs. Welsh's portrayal of John Duncan. "How did he take this all in?"

"Oh, that poor wreck of a soul," Mrs. Welsh sighed. Gossip, even from a hundred years ago, still titillated. "People said he ran himself into a shadow of a man, the way he fell for that woman. Some say his family forbid him to walk in the same wind with Mary Ann. He was too good for her, they said. He kept himself behind closed doors for years. He had money, but it didn't put a spark in Mary Ann. She outright turned him down because his family would have disowned him if the marriage had been tied up in a knot."

"Then why were they buried so close together?" Willow asked.

"The gravediggers liked the old man," Mrs. Welsh replied. "Felt sorry for him. They saw to it that he was buried beside her. I don't think they knew the real story, but they knew there wasn't a darn thing she could do about his presence now."

Willow smiled at the thought of Mary Ann's provocative eye, sowing fear into the hearts of the men who loved her to make them keep their distance, the boldness that rested under an inexplicable bouquet of flowers. Willow knew that the strange set of circumstances that had placed them side by side in death would always be as mysterious as the life people imagined they had.

===

CHAPTER SEVENTEEN

Slow Waltz

On Monday morning, water pooled in puddles as brown as dead moths as Willow walked to work. She had not heard the rain falling through the night, or if she had, she'd paid little attention to it. Her mind was still on Mary Ann and the mysterious bouquet. Who caters to the dead after so many years?

Once Willow was in the office, the intercom buzzed, and Dr. Millhouse's voice came through the receiver like words seeping through a crack in a wall. "I'll be in to check up on your mother this afternoon. Her sight is dimming. I think the tumour is getting close to the optic nerve."

Willow didn't answer him. He was monitoring her mother's illness like a weatherman tracking a hurricane. He steered death in his own direction and pawed at it like a cat with a mouse until its demise. She glanced at him through the open door of his office. He had an hour before he'd see his first patient. He sat at his desk, which was snarled in papers, and rocked back and forth to a rhythm that entertained something on his mind. A low-burning light bulb hung from the ceiling above his desk, giving off a yellow glow that made him look like an old cleric searching for meaning in an ancient script. Some women patients didn't like the doctor. They complained he told them they sought illness in the refuge of their minds, which soured their husband's taste for them. Willow knew many women left the office with eyes reddened by tears spilled under that light bulb. Some of them coughed to fake a cold. Others mentioned, as they left the office, that pink eye ran in the family.

"Take care of yourself!" waiting patients often called out as another upset woman stormed out of the doctor's office.

Nearing lunch hour, Willow went into the kitchenette off the waiting room and plugged in the kettle. She would make a pot of tea for Dr. Millhouse and place it on his desk with his favourite deep mug. She would set out the silver tray for his wife as well. She placed two cups and saucers— one for her and one for Kathleen—beside the teapot on the silver tray. This was the highlight of her working day, her tea visits with Kathleen Millhouse. They had become like sisters over the years.

Kathleen smiled when Willow brought in the tray. "How are you today, Willow? I hope you are getting enough sleep."

"May I ask you something personal, Kathleen?" Willow asked, before turning her face away from her friend.

"Yes, of course you can, as long as you face me eye to eye. I don't question the air, and neither do you."

Willow turned and faced her smiling friend. "There is no cure for your illness, Kathleen. You know it, your husband knows it." Willow swallowed deeply. "How do you think Dr. Millhouse will do on his own?"

"Ah, my dear friend, you are asking if he will survive. I have been counselling him for quite a while on the same question. What you are really asking me is if *you* will survive what is facing you once again."

"And what does he say, Kathleen?"

"As you might have guessed, not a word. He believes that if he agrees with what I'm saying, it's my password to let go and pass on with his permission. People know death's power but would rather cling to the vine of hopelessness in life." Kathleen paused, then softened her voice. "Your mother is not aware of her illness most days. Who knows what she may glimpse into the past, remembering her wedding night or the birth of her child? These are powerful emotions. I, for one, believe emotions are the brain's fuel. You will survive. You are stronger than many, many people I've known. You've always been a helper. You're not a needy person, Willow."

‡ ‡ ‡

THAT NIGHT, HER mother was sitting upright in bed when Willow returned from work. She listened to her mother's voice crying out from the bedroom, while Mrs. Welsh stood at the stove folding her hands over and over.

"She's been calling out to your father all day long. I don't know what to say to her," she told Willow, her voice full of concern. "She's got a conversation going on with him. I feel like I'm standing between the living and the dead. My mother told us about the haunted houses in Glenmor. She said the dead come back if they've left something unfinished here on earth. Or if they owe money to someone. I can't figure out how they'd pay the money back, though."

Willow's head ached. "Tell her he's working on something, Mrs. Welsh," she said with a sigh. "Tell her he has to finish something. That usually calms her down." She grabbed a bottle of Aspirin and swallowed three.

"She says your father comes to her every night. Brings her new eyes." Mrs. Welsh hastily blessed herself. "Sweet Jesus, I'm telling myself, this house is haunted. I liked your father very much, a prince of a man he was in life, but it terrifies me to think that he returns from the grave."

"The doctor will be over to see her later," Willow said. "I'll have to make a decision before winter arrives. I'll have to put her in the hospital sooner or later."

Mrs. Welsh removed her apron and hung it on a hook in the pantry. "I don't mean to complain, but she scares the devil out of me, talking to the dead like he was standing right there, listening to her every word."

"I'll sleep on the cot near her, Mrs. Welsh. You can sleep in your own bed tonight." Willow exhaled, head pounding.

Mrs. Welsh's face relaxed. She was a little worried that Willow might tell her not to bother coming back. She hated to think about money at a time like this, but she did have a new coat ordered from the Eaton's catalogue. Cash on delivery. She'd be mortified if she had to ask the postmistress to hold it until her monthly cheque came in. She'd already told people she got a full hand every week for her work. Willow was good to pay her every Friday. Handed over the cash like candy. These people weren't misers.

Mrs. Welsh went home for the night, if only to escape the ghosts temporarily.

After she left, Willow brought her mother a small bowl of porridge. Nothing else passed her lips these days. Porridge was the only food she could recognize at this stage of her illness. She couldn't distinguish a piece of bread from a pat of butter.

Her mother was aware of someone's presence in the room, and reached out her hands for a touch.

"I brought your porridge, Mother."

Willow sat beside her bed. A small white hand stroked Willow's face, like a child's hand seeking familiar bones, a deep dimple, a mouth with a secret smile just for her. Willow turned her head towards the wall. There was something startling about watching someone disappear before your eyes. The first thing to be claimed was the true colour of the eyes, something dim left in its place. The bones then shed their flesh. And when her mother stood up to dance, her feet had forgotten the steps.

"I've brought you your favourite. It's porridge," Willow repeated.

"Nobody comes to visit me. I never see anyone any-more."

"Lots of people come to see you, Mother. Mrs. Welsh told me four people dropped by today."

"I didn't see a soul."

"Are you hungry? The doctor will be in later on to check on you."

"Give it to that doctor! He always looks hungry."

"I'll take you for a little walk around the kitchen after you eat. And I'll put on some music for you."

Later, Willow led her by the hand to the kitchen. A warm fire lent the room its heat. Willow turned on the radio. A slow waltz made Rhona smile. Her face lit up as they sang to each other, Rhona's childlike voice on the rim of the power-ful voice of her daughter.

Their singing was interrupted by the sound of shuffling on the front step, followed by the swing and slam of the screen door. Dr. Millhouse walked into the room. He was earlier than usual this evening.

"Let her finish her song." His voice was thin, diluted by fatigue. "Have you given her a pain pill today?"

"I give her one before I go to work in the morning."

"Her eyes are bloodshot."

Willow carried her singing mother back to bed and went into the pantry. She knew what he was going to say when he looked at her from the pantry doorway.

"There's no more I can do for her here at home. I suspect she has a small bleed in the brain now. She will need much heavier medication, which they can provide in the hospital."

Willow forced herself to look at Dr. Millhouse, who was standing a foot away from her. His eyes were red and weary from too little sleep. His voice crawled like a cold hand seeking warmth over a fire.

"I'll call to have her admitted by Saturday. It'll give you time to get things in order. The ambulance should be available. You can leave early in the morning."

Willow looked out the pantry window. She didn't hear him leave. He was gone when she turned back and looked at the doorway.

‡ ‡ ‡

THE NEXT DAY, Willow began to pack her mother's suitcase, leaving out only a few personal items, things she knew Rhona would no longer need—jewellery, art supplies, most of her clothes. Mrs. Welsh wept into a tissue as she gave details of her own mother's passing in the hospital.

"My mother passed away in the butt of winter. Snow

covered half the windows. People came to the wake like ghosts and melted beside the stove before going into the parlour to see her. Me and my sisters kept the mop going for three days and nights straight. It was awful. I wanted to bury myself in a snowbank until spring. It took twelve men to dig her grave."

Willow bit her bottom lip and listened patiently to Mrs. Welsh's misery. The story seemed to go on forever. "Thank heavens Glenmor has a funeral parlour these days," Willow said to distract her. "As you know, that's where my father was waked."

"Oh, but dear, it's not the same as being home. Their spirit is here. I believe it takes days before their spirit leaves the home. People believe they will come back to finish what was left undone."

Willow smiled. She never believed the dead would ever need to come back for anything. Or were the bearers of gifts to a loved one.

‡ ‡ ‡

AFTER SHE FINISHED packing, Willow brought her mother another bowl of porridge. Rhona turned in her bed as Willow approached. "Is this day or nighttime?"

"It's daytime, Mother. I brought you a bowl of porridge." Willow turned her face towards the wall. "You'll be going for a ride Saturday morning."

"Where am I going? I'm too tired to go very far. My head has been aching for years now. My husband gives me Aspirins, but they don't work."

"You're going to a place where they will take your head-aches away."

Rhona looked up at her daughter. "I can't stay there too long. Your father will miss me."

"They have stronger Aspirins there, Mother. You will be fine and everyone will visit you."

"Will there be snow there?"

"No snow, Mother."

Willow heard sobs from the kitchen and the rattling of teacups. She removed the painting of the blue jay from the wall and tucked it carefully into the suitcase.

‡ ‡ ‡

ON SATURDAY MORNING, the wind smeared the air with a low howl, and the sky was jammed with grey clouds. Rhona Alexander, wrapped in a warm blanket, lay on the stretcher. Black straps were securely tugged into place. A paramedic placed dark glasses over Rhona's eyes, as Willow and Mrs. Welsh stood beside her. Willow noticed how pale her mother was in the full light of day. She saw the blue of her mother's lips as small talk increased back and forth. Rhona asked for her green shawl.

"It feels like something's about to fall on me," she whispered. "Ask your husband, Willow. Ask Graham if he knows what's wrong with me and to make me feel better."

Willow sank her teeth into her bottom lip as the ambulance moved slowly down the lane and took a left turn to the highway. Willow followed, her hands damp on the wheel of her car. Mrs. Welsh had looked over the contents of the suitcase before they left. Everything was in place. She didn't mention the painting of the blue jay, thinking it was probably a childhood painting included by Willow as a gesture of affection for her dying mother.

When they reached the second winding turn on the mountain highway, the ambulance's red light flashed suddenly as it came to a full stop on the side of the road. Willow pulled up behind the blinking vehicle.

The driver motioned for Willow to wait as he walked around the ambulance and opened the back door. Willow could see the paramedic leaning over the stretcher. An oxygen mask covered her mother's face. The other attendant began talking into a hand-held radio. Mrs. Welsh began praying out loud, begging God to let them make it to the hospital. Willow and Mrs. Welsh got out of the car and stood at the back door of the ambulance to find out what was going on.

"She went into cardiac arrest," the driver said. "We tried everything we could. I'm sorry for your loss. Dr. Millhouse is on his way."

Willow climbed into the back of the ambulance. She

recognized the face of death when she removed the oxygen mask. An undisputable look of radiant peace covered her mother's pale face. Willow had seen this look on her mother's face before, when she walked up the stairs of the church with Willow on the day of her wedding. Rhona had looked beautiful enough to be the bride.

Rhona Cropper Alexander was pronounced dead at 9:13 a.m. It was October 1979. Not quite four years after her husband's death.

Willow buried her mother beside her father three days after her passing. Her funeral was crowded. People both known and unknown to Willow made an appearance. Some spoke in whispers. Others found stories to share, in respectful tones, with the people beside them. The Alexanders were well-liked in Glenmor.

Two of her father's sisters came to the funeral and left shortly after. The other was somewhere in South America. Their embraces were more like grips on Willow, as if they had rehearsed on a mannequin. Willow could tell by the look in their eyes that they were uneasy. They liked her mother and said the right things and asked Willow not to be a stranger at their door. Willow didn't dislike her father's family; she just resented the fact that her father had sacrificed his education to allow them to succeed. But they adored their big brother, and they were more like her father than she thought.

Willow had hoped Marjorie, her only friend, could

make it to the funeral. She'd even offered to buy a return ticket for her. And Marjorie did make it, arriving with her parents in a shiny new truck. As soon as they saw Willow, they whisked her into their arms in a bear hug.

"Our home is your home, dear. You know where to find us," said Alma as they were leaving.

Marjorie announced to Willow that she would be returning to the mountain in the spring and was finally going to rebuild on the old family property. The girls hugged each other, wiping back tears. Marjorie swore she'd have a haystack of clothes in her hall for old times' sake.

Eventually, it was the whip and lash of heavy rain that drove people away from the funeral. At the cemetery, arrows of lightning appeared to be aiming at the tombstones. Angry thunder exploded between the trees. When it stopped, Willow stood alone beside the open book of her parents' tombstone and watched a heavy mist erase their names.

Dr. Millhouse arrived at Willow's door three hours after the funeral to deliver sleeping pills in a brown envelope. "You may need these, Willow. Trying times require trying pills and a good rest." He didn't enter the house. "I want you to take a couple of weeks off from work."

After the doctor left, Willow curled up in her chair and hoped for no more visitors. She placed Henry beside her chair. Now she'd have all the silence she needed.

CHAPTER EIGHTEEN

==

A Mile of Grief

WILLOW RETURNED TO WORK A COUPLE OF weeks after her mother's death. On her first day back, she decided to walk the mile to work, even though a naked Monday morning sky predicted inclement weather. Willow faced the new day in a grey dress and oxfords from her closet. Passing the full-length mirror, she looked at herself briefly and thought she resembled a strip of pleated fog. She planned to go on a shopping trip on the weekend. She wanted to introduce colour back into her life—a touch of green, soft yellows, sky blues to brighten her days. She and Kathleen had gone over colour charts. They both chose the same colours.

"Grief can rob you of so much, Willow. Don't let it near your rainbow. You are a beautiful woman. Keep colour in your life!"

It didn't surprise Willow how many of Dr. Millhouse's

patients offered their condolences while awaiting diagnosis of their ailments. But their sympathy didn't stop there. Many of them thought that talking about their own dead relatives might somehow help Willow. They dug up their own dead and reanimated them in trivial rambles.

"My grandfather loved the fall," declared one. "He danced with the scarecrows, my dear, before he retired them to the barn. He died a terrible death under his tractor. They found an arm and a leg in the potato patch. He is dancing with the angels now. There are no seasons in heaven."

"My mother dropped dead in church," said an elderly woman. "Some people believe she saw a vision and fainted. But it was dead she was, stone dead on her knees. People believe if you die in church the gates of heaven are left open for you—no passport required at the gate."

"Your mother and father were the salt of the earth," many others said.

It was their way of connecting their pain and misery with hers—a gentle competition and something to be grateful for if the body died in one piece. It didn't help Willow one bit, but she still thanked the elderly people for their words of sympathy.

She was relieved each day when the clock struck twelve and the office was empty. She made tea to take upstairs to Kathleen. She had a special treat for her today: inside the round tin can was her favourite chocolate cake with boiled frosting.

Kathleen Millhouse was propped up in bed and smiled up at Willow when she entered the room. She lived between pillows these days, positioned on each side of her thin body. Except for her soft-spoken voice, you would have thought you were looking down upon a corpse with a welcoming smile on its lips. Her hands were folded in a criss-cross of cold flesh. A head of coal-black waves rolled out over the pillows.

Her misty eyes, as round as quarters, studied Willow's face. Willow knew what she sought. Kathleen's body was dying slowly, but her mind had yet to surrender to the illness of multiple sclerosis. She was in her early fifties. She didn't speak to angels or ask for a pardon from death. Willow had always been drawn into the deep intellectual caves Kathleen explored. She had travelled the world and spoke a half-dozen languages. She was a Harvard graduate with a degree in psychology that had turned yellow on the wall.

"MS in itself is not fatal," she had informed Willow when they'd first met years earlier. "The complications from it can be the culprit. My support workers have turned me into a waltzing Matilda. I walk along the balcony two or three times a day—a few more when the weather is warmer. One must not lie flat for too long."

She came to Glenmor a few months after Dr. Millhouse's arrival. He had a balcony built for her leisure, along with a ramp for her wheelchair. They had no children. She was originally from Manitoba, but confessed to Willow, "I love the sea. There's magic in every wave that samples the sand. I prefer to believe that secrets roll out with the waves. I'm not a religious person; magic is for dreamers and children. That's why I suggested to James this would be the perfect place to live."

In the bedroom, there was a wedding photo on the dresser. Kathleen was wearing a blue organza dress flowing to her ankles, and she held a bouquet of daisies in one hand. One daisy was pinned behind her right ear. Dr. Millhouse was in a plaid jacket and grey dress pants. The daisy in his lapel was wilted. He had no beard or moustache on his wedding day. He looked like a character from a television sitcom. His smile was pleasant towards Kathleen.

Willow placed the rolling tray within Kathleen's reach and set a cup of tea and a slice of cake in front of her.

"How are you doing, Willow?" Kathleen lifted her fork delicately.

"Everything is taken care of. The bills are paid. My mother left enough money behind. She never really spent much of her father's inheritance."

"I'm glad to hear that, Willow. But what I meant was, how are you dealing with life itself? I know what trauma can do to a person. A long vacation would do you the world of good. It's the world's best therapy."

Willow didn't respond. She didn't want a vacation. She just wanted to be in the Alexander house surrounded by its familiar sounds and scents. Sounds released memories for her. The shrill cry of the wind in the eaves was like abandoned angels singing at heaven's gate, begging to be allowed back inside. That's what her mother believed whenever she heard the wind crying. Her mother said she wasn't sure what the angels had done to anger heaven. Willow preferred to imagine the angels storming the gate, their voices shrill and demanding, only to be silenced by the gatekeeper.

What Willow wished to hear now were footsteps coming up to the screen door. Her father always stopped and removed his boots or shoes before coming into the house. He would tap them gently against the edge of the step and enter as quietly as a cat. She also wished to hear the swift shuffling of cards, and the bang of fists on the card table from a winning hand. Or the swish of lemonade over ice, sounding like a gentle waterfall. On cold mornings she'd listened to the rage of a winter fire racing up the chimney in her bedroom. She also longed for familiar smells. The smell of hot chocolate warming the chilled air that took her from sleep. She also loved the smell of paint coming from her mother's brushes. Willow believed it was possible to smell colours then.

Willow had thought of visiting Marjorie, who now lived in Boston. But the idea vaporized with the news that Marjorie had a case of shingles. She would be in no shape to visit with Willow and show her around. Willow wanted to explore the city, look for Cropper graves. Her grandmother's headstone was on her list of things to find. She knew Judge Cropper's headstone, with a gavel etched in marble, was next to Edith's. She wondered what was carved on Edith's stone. A magic wand? Her mother never did go back to Boston to visit her parents' graves. She had always been afraid of flying. Her father had once offered to drive her there.

"No, Murdoch," Rhona had said, "my nerves couldn't take the heavy traffic. The trucks would run us down like squirrels. It's no wonder city people come home from work and lock themselves in until the next morning. The poor souls. They can't stand the traffic."

Perhaps Marjorie would be up to sightseeing after she recovered. Willow knew Marjorie would be happy to travel to different parts of the world with her. She and her husband had divorced after two years of a childless marriage. He smoked two packs of cigarettes a day, which he said was due to the stress of his heavy workload.

"Ma said he was a fire hazard. And you know how afraid of fires I am since our house burned down," Marjorie had once said to Willow.

Willow sympathized with her friend.

"And besides," Marjorie added, "kissing him was like kissing a coal stove with the lid open."

Her husband died a month after the divorce.

CHAPTER NINETEEN

<hr>

A Voice in the Rain

M AY OF 1985 WAS DAMP AND CLEAN. NEW LEAVES shimmered from a rain bath. Greens buds burst on the tips of naked branches filled with homecoming birds. At times Willow could hear her mother's voice in the rain. It was usually late at night, when something interrupted her sleep. She could hear her mother singing the song she always sang on Willow's birthday, about bluebirds.

The day before her fortieth birthday, years after the deaths of her parents, Willow was not looking for bluebirds. Yet, unexpectedly, they appeared. Or were they a dream? Willow worried the birds might be a warning. Something was going happen tomorrow, on her birthday.

When she awoke that morning, she counted a cluster of six stars in the pre-dawn sky. She put on her rubber boots and went out to her father's workshop. Everything in the workshop was the same and still in its place. Nothing had been moved since he died. The silent lathe stood full of dust. The electric tools were off to one side, each tucked in its own space, on deep built-in shelves like tombs. Hammers and handsaws hung according to size on the back wall. An orange power saw sat upon a wooden bench, its steel blade shining like crude silver teeth. What she'd loved most as a child was the way her father displayed the nails. He fastened the lids of empty bottles to a wooden board and then filled the bottles with nails before screwing the lids back on. They still hung from the beam above his work table.

In the right corner, next to the door, the old nursery rocker stood. Her mother had made a cushion for the seat, a cross-stitch pattern of a child chasing a running dog down a road. It was still clear enough to make out the child's hand reaching for the dog's outstretched tail. The dog had a rag doll in a blue dress in its mouth. This had been Willow's seat as a child, where she would often sit and watch her father at work, safely away from the saw blade, as he always insisted.

Cobwebs grew along the wooden ceiling. "A spider's garden," Willow thought as her eyes followed the pattern of webs. She would ask Mrs. Welsh to have her sons remove the contents of the workshop for their own use. They were all carpenters. Two mice ran along the dusty floor.

The irony of the mice being alive was not lost on Willow. Kathleen and James Millhouse were dead. Now

Willow was worried the autopsy reports would reveal rat poison in their blood.

Willow tried to remember the sequence of events that day. She had taken the poison from under the sink in the morning to sprinkle in her father's workshop. It was in a jar. Her mother always put everything into jars because she believed they lost their strength if they were left in boxes. She labelled the jars many years ago, but the words had faded. At the time, Willow was distracted by other things. She put the jar down on the counter, then decided to make strawberry shortcake for the Millhouses.

She pictured the scene in her head: The rat poison sitting by the sink. The jar of baking powder next to it. Both white powder. Could she have used the wrong powder? Did she use both of them?

Willow is sure she is going to be charged with murder. Who is going to believe it was a mistake? How could she have been that careless? How would she ever explain her terrible mistake? Most people knew how close she and Dr. Millhouse's wife had become. The housekeeper, Irene, could certainly vouch for that.

Willow made a mental list of things she had to do before the police came for her. She decided to place family photos—her personal and beloved keepsakes—in a box and have Mrs. Welsh take it away for safekeeping. She would ask her to take Henry as well. Willow did not want to leave any personal items in the empty house for strangers to destroy after she was gone.

Willow recalled the letter Graham had written to her after her mother's death. She'd burned it in the stove. She had laughed out loud when she read how sorry he was for her loss, how he was coming back to Glenmor to practise medicine alone. In the letter, he made a point of saying that he was newly divorced. He even had the nerve to say he should never have left the mountain. "I didn't want my return to be a surprise," Graham wrote. "I thought you had a right to know."

Had he really expected a reply? "How wonderful of you to introduce your reappearance," she had thought of penning. "Your broken marriage. And your regrets on leaving the mountain. A litany of mortal scars scrawled in red ink— how repentant of you. You have no idea what awaits you . . ."

CHAPTER TWENTY

Tea in a China Cup

WILLOW HAS NO PHOTOS OF JAMES AND KATHleen Millhouse. She only has the memories that fill her troubled nights, when her nightmares are more frequent. At every window, Kathleen and James are looking in at her, calling out for Willow to return the pink pearl necklace Kathleen gave to her before she died. They want to know why she killed them.

Willow recalls how Kathleen ate the cake with her tea that evening while she visited, Kathleen's frail hand struggling to hold the teacup, her speech interrupted by small pants for breath. Willow remembers Kathleen telling her to make sure James had some cake too.

"And tell him I want him to drink his tea from a china cup," she said.

Willow was putting the leftovers into the fridge downstairs when she heard the doctor call her from the bottom of the stairs.

"Willow, can you come into the office?"

Willow entered his office and placed the plate of strawberry shortcake on his desk. Willow mentioned Kathleen's shallow breathing to him, but he didn't respond. He didn't ask why she had dropped in for an evening visit, even though she'd never done so before. But she knew that time was running out for Kathleen, and she'd wanted to bring her the gift of the cake.

"I know Kathleen has pneumonia," Willow said to Dr. Millhouse. "Her condition is worsening."

The doctor was slow to meet her gaze. When he finally looked up at Willow, his face was flushed and his eyes were as bloodshot as a junkyard hound's. It was clear he'd been drinking. That *was* a surprise to Willow. She had never seen him drink before.

"Did she tell you what day this is?" His tone was flat.

Willow swallowed hard but didn't respond.

"It's our wedding anniversary," he said. "I thought that's why you brought over the cake. We ate strawberry shortcake on our wedding day. Kathleen must have told you. As folly will allow on such occasions, friends showered us with strawberry oven mitts and dishtowels and aprons as gifts to complement the damn cake."

"Kathleen never mentioned it to me. I had no idea."

"You are a very perceptive woman, Willow. Brilliant to the roots of your wisdom teeth. Perhaps you should have been a doctor. Sometimes you remind me of myself. No emotions to spare either. That young Currie boy was quite bright too. Too bad he was raised by a woman like his mother. I hope he has learned to unsaddle himself from female persuasions." And, in a lower voice, he asked her a question. "I know you were his first love. Don't give up on it. Were you in love with him?"

"Yes," Willow answered, surprising herself with such a quick response.

"Good. It will hit you again when you least expect it. I'm sure that's what the poor boy is waiting for. He's a man now. He was a boy when he left and married. Give him a chance to prove it. I don't know why in hell he stayed married for ten years to that woman. I strongly believe that there was some noose being held over his head. She's as mad as a hatter. I met her in Halifax a couple of times. I believe he has matured and become the man you always wanted and needed."

Willow bristled at the discussion of Graham and remained silent.

"Did I ever tell you that your father was one of the most brilliant men I've ever met?"

"I believe you have," Willow replied.

"He understood life as well as death. He never feared physical death—or the afterlife, for that matter. That is rare in a man." Dr. Millhouse paused, as though caught short by some internal jolt. Then he continued. "Myself, I am no more than an emotional imposter. My wife lies above my head while death counts the breaths she has left. She is free from all illness in her mind. She has the same mindset as your father had. And I am terrified of living without her. The damn world is barren without someone to love. You know the feelings I'm talking about, Willow."

Willow poured him a cup of strong, steaming tea and pushed it across the desk towards him. "Kathleen asked me to make sure you had a piece of cake and a cup of tea in a china cup."

Dr. Millhouse took a few slurps of tea. A flock of sea-gulls perched on the fence outside, screeching. "Freedom is a wonderful thing. Listen to them! I believe your God put voices into the wrong creatures. I suspect they are trying to tell us something," said Dr. Millhouse.

A few days earlier, he had turned his head away when he announced to Willow that he would have to terminate her employment in a week's time. "I have urgent issues to attend to at the moment."

Willow hadn't answered him. She was relieved. Some time off was what she needed. She assumed the reason for Dr. Millhouse's decision was Kathleen's declining health. Willow was happy he was taking time off to be with her. Old Doc Morrison was still in good health and would fill in for a few weeks. His wife would work in the office with him, so Willow would have time off too.

Willow poured a cup of tea for herself and listened to the doctor ramble on. She had never been particularly fond of him, but she still felt sympathy as he tried to come to terms with his wife's impending death. Dr. Millhouse told her that Kathleen had wanted to die in her old home, but it was too late to grant her last request. He looked so bereft at this disclosure that Willow wanted to reach over her cup and touch his hand. He was in a most vulnerable state. But she held back because she knew that he didn't want her pity, no more than he'd wanted oven mitts dotted with strawberries for a wedding gift. She was simply a listening post, someone who knew and respected his beloved Kathleen. Perhaps he also confided in her because she was his old friend Murdoch Alexander's daughter.

"I was reared by an old grandmother who should have died ten years before she did," Dr. Millhouse continued. "My parents and only sibling were killed when I was eight. Old Granny, my father's mother, stayed alive to keep me under her roof until I went to college. Then one day she took off her apron and hung it on a hook in the pantry, and said, 'That's it for me. You are on your own, boy.'" He paused. "I knew it was the end of the line. She was ninety, smoked a pipe and believed hell lit its torch from the flames of Mother Earth." He released a slow breath. "Do you believe in the afterlife, Willow?"

"I believe good people like my mother and father and Kathleen will be rewarded."

"What about people like me, Willow? What's waiting for me?"

"Oh, I believe you will be greeted by a flock of seagulls and dear Kathleen with a smile on her face. She won't let you fly away."

"You are a good woman, Willow. Now go and love the hell out of life. You deserve it!" He looked down at the slice of cake on his desk as Willow got up to leave.

‡ ‡ ‡

THE BARE LIGHT bulb over Dr. Millhouse's desk was still burning when Willow arrived at the clinic the next morning to check on Kathleen. It cast a dull yellow glare over the gruesome scene that greeted her. Dr. Millhouse sat in his chair, slumped over the desk, his right arm propped up, a fork gripped in his hand. A few crumbs of cake were lodged between the tines. His eyes were half-closed like an aging actor in his final scene, closing out the light of a new day.

Willow phoned Doc Morrison before she raced up the stairs to check on Kathleen. She was still knocking on Kathleen's door when the doctor arrived. They entered the room together. Willow looked down at Kathleen Millhouse's still, cold body. The black waves of her hair sprawled against her pillow. Doc Morrison checked her pulse and shook his head. Willow pulled from her handbag a piece of blue ribbon she had saved from her silk kite and tied back Kathleen's hair. The dead woman's face, under her high cheekbones, was a pale mauve. She was smiling. A smile left over, Willow liked to think, from her last words with her husband.

Earlier that week, Kathleen had asked Willow to open the top drawer of her dresser and take out a gold box. "You've been a wonderful friend," she said, holding up a strand of pink pearls. "These were my aunt's. I want you to have them."

At the time, Kathleen had tried to tell Willow something else. But her speech was fractured and her breath uneven. "There'll be big changes . . . in your life . . . Willow. James believes it is time for us . . . Graham . . . coming home . . . You will find peace . . ." Her voice floated into a whisper.

Willow had asked Kathleen not to continue talking; she was using too much of her precious energy. But Willow understood what she was trying to say. She could fill in the blanks.

Most people knew very little about the personal life of the doctor and his wife after they arrived in the village. Kathleen's illness kept her a stranger to almost everyone. Some of the villagers had never seen her in person. Others suspected the doctor kept her secluded because she suffered from a secret mental illness. Many had seen her on the balcony from a distance, but they said she never returned their wave. They thought Kathleen Millhouse looked like a princess who was forbidden to respond to the fish-scaled or balsam-stained hands of ordinary people. There would be gossip and stories about Kathleen and Dr. Millhouse for a long time to come after their deaths, Willow was sure of that.

It was Irene, who had to leave early one day, who had first asked Willow if she had time to bring a cup of tea to Mrs. Millhouse. "She likes it well brewed and in a china cup," she'd said. "I know you can make a good cup of tea." Willow had been working there for a week and was happy to meet the mysterious Kathleen Millhouse.

It was not an imposition for Willow. Like everyone else, she was curious about Kathleen and her condition. When Willow entered her room that first day, Kathleen was sitting up in bed. Her face was flushed, with a deep dimple on either side of her smile.

"It's so nice to finally meet you, Willow," she said softly. "Irene said you'd be up shortly."

"I hope you enjoy the tea. I'm a china-cup person myself, Mrs. Millhouse."

"It's Kathleen, and I already know how handy you are around the kitchen."

They both chuckled after discussing the trivial conversations people engage in at first meetings.

"I'm usually loud and inquisitive." Kathleen laughed, holding out her hand.

"I'm usually reserved and alone," Willow replied.

"I like you, Willow. I'm sure you and I will enjoy many conversations. Why don't you become my regular tea

server? I can have Irene leave at noon. Would that be agree-
able to you?"

Willow smiled. "Of course. I doubt Irene will mind. It'll
give her a chance to take her clothes off the line. She'll have
them ironed before we finish our tea."

"She is a dear. A joy to have around," Kathleen replied.

It frightens Willow now that she can't remember
Kathleen Millhouse's last conversation with her. She
remembers only her smile, her mouth slightly open, revealing the edge of her pearly-white teeth. It wasn't a pained
smile or one troubled by an uncomfortable word. It had a
calmness, as though she was ready for sleep.

After he'd examined the bodies, old Dr. Morrison
turned towards Willow. "James called me last night and said
Kathleen was doing poorly. He said she was sleeping, and
he was having a cup of tea. There was no reason for me
to come over. He seemed a bit distressed, but I knew he
could take care of things. Perhaps I should have visited to
check things out." He took a deep breath, then went on. "If
she was strong enough, they were planning on leaving next
week. She wanted to die out west, in her old home."

Willow remained silent, recalling how the doctor had
said there wasn't enough time left to get Kathleen to the
old house.

"James adored Kathleen," Doc Morrison mused. "The
poor man's heart must have just given out from the sorrow.
He knew she would not live long." He was visibly shaken.

Then he casually added: "I assume you're aware that young Graham Currie is taking over the practice. He inquired about the clinic when he was home not that long after your father passed away. He came to visit me and said he had to put in a few more years before he could leave New York."

The words about Graham were too much for Willow to process at that moment. When the police officers arrived on the scene at the Millhouse clinic, they didn't ask to speak to her, so she left. As she walked out, two emergency vehicles were parked in front, their lights brightening up the cool, dull day with an icy glare. A few villagers had gathered to gawk. Someone asked Willow what was going on.

She didn't respond. She just kept walking towards home.

CHAPTER TWENTY-ONE

The Long Road Home

As Graham Currie travelled closer to Glenmor, he felt like a man released from himself. Everything seemed familiar to him, yet distant against time. He watched a wave of gulls crashing out from behind the old breakwater as he drove along. The sudden flashes of the trees trembling on the mountainside waved for his attention like lost children. The sea bathed the last of summer feet—lovers caught up in the white, thick foam of a bubble-bath sea.

On his return, Graham knew he would see for himself what was left of Willow Alexander's life. And his own. They were both forty now. He was anxious to see her deep-green eyes and her flowing fire mane. He thought he might find her at the gravesite of her parents, where she might wander off to Mary Ann's grave. He still thought warmly of his mountain lover, his first and only love.

He recalled his own misgivings at their wedding rehearsal. The look in her eyes. Her slow movements as she walked down the aisle, her arms at her sides. The paleness of her face should have alerted him to something. Her father walked beside her with his hands folded in front of him. She'd looked directly into Graham's eyes at the end of her walk, asking a question without speaking. Did she suspect something? Women have a way of figuring things out with their intuition. He recalled the way she smiled at him when she drove away from the rehearsal with her parents.

Afterwards, he had expected her to withdraw from their marriage plans and wait for him. How he wished she had seen through him at the rehearsal and postponed the wedding until he'd finished medical school and started up a practice in Glenmor. If he had got up the nerve to knock on Murdoch Alexander's door, where would he be now? If he had dealt with things differently, would he have fought off the threats of Polina Rebane—her claim she had been taken advantage of when Graham Currie came to visit her apartment? There was a dark rainbow of bruises on her thighs, caused by him during the assault she alleged. How would his supervisor have handled the complaint against him? She claimed he drank her whiskey like water before attacking her, then left the next morning with an alley cat folded under his arm. She'd watched him leave from her bedroom window.

Polina made several visits to see Graham after that night, before she had to go back to New York.

"I can make things easier for you," she had told him. "We can marry here. The papers will be a cinch to process. It will be easy for you to get into America with an American wife."

She said all this in an empty cafeteria while Graham watched through the window as a lone maple tree gave up its last leaves to the passing wind, letting them drop like wrinkled paper onto a park bench. Graham rose from his chair and said he was going back to work. Instead, he dashed out a side door and made his way home to his small ground-floor apartment and Whiskey Jack, the alley cat. Whiskey demanded to be fed, and curled at Graham's ankles as soon as he opened the door. After he ate, the cat jumped outside through the window that Graham always left open so he could come and go as he pleased.

The memories ripped open the scars that still remained thinly veiled under his skin. How could Willow not have known something was up before the wedding? She had always been smarter than he was. Graham regretted not confiding in her or her father before he allowed Polina to ruin the next ten years of his life.

‡ ‡ ‡

GRAHAM AND POLINA were married in Halifax by a Justice of the Peace in 1974, after Graham completed his internship and residency. No family from either side attended. That was the way Graham had planned it. A blackmail wedding needed no congratulations. He invited his father to spend some time with him in Halifax after the marriage, before he left for New York. He introduced Polina to his father as Dr. Rebane. Mr. Currie nodded in her direction. He didn't shake her hand. No welcome-to-the-family speech. He disliked her on sight. Graham picked up Whiskey Jack and rubbed his fur. Polina offered to get some takeout food and left Graham alone with his father.

"I shall not be long, my darling husband, and father-in-law," she said as she left.

Polina let nothing bother her once they were married: the fact that Graham told her to use her maiden name; the fact that his father's face went sour when he saw her; the fact that her husband refused to wear the wedding ring she'd bought him. She had bought her own wedding band as well. It was silver, with the initials *P* and *G* carved on the inside. The fact that Graham never made love to her she put down to fatigue. All she cared about was that she was a married woman with a husband and a career. She had planned and executed this union. Someday, he would thank her for saving his career, she thought. As his wife, she could not testify against him in court, if she accused him of attacking her and taking her money. She viewed their marriage as a peace offering, an olive branch. Whereas Graham saw it for what it was, a trap. But Polina could accuse him of nothing now. His career had been spared at her expense. "All is fair in love and war," she reminded herself as she strolled to the Chinese restaurant to pick up some food for Graham and her new father-in-law.

"What's going on here, Graham?" Mr. Currie asked when Polina was gone. His white face against the black sheen of Whiskey Jack's fur looked as though it were made of plaster. "You left the lovely Willow Alexander at the altar for this woman? I don't trust her, Graham." Mr. Currie had seen something in her small, greedy eyes that frightened him.

Graham broke down and wept openly. "I didn't have a choice. She threatened to accuse me of rape and ruin my career. My life with Willow would've been over. My career would've been destroyed before it even began. How could I ever return to Glenmor and practise medicine if she made her accusations public? The night that it happened, I went over to her apartment, at her request, to bring her some notes I'd prepared for her research. I drank some whiskey she gave me. I remember nothing else. But I know I never touched her, then or since."

Mr. Currie sat at the table with his head in his hands. His shoulders shook. He turned and looked at Graham. "You believed marrying her would keep her silent. You should have told Willow what was happening."

"Dad, I went back to the Alexander property twice the night of the rehearsal, hoping Murdoch was in his workshop so I could talk to him. I was going mad over the state

I was in. I believed she was better off without me after the fool I made of myself and our relationship, and I left."

"They would have helped you, Graham. Murdoch Alexander is a wise man. I want to talk to Willow, let her know what happened."

"Please, Dad, not a word to her. I want to be man enough to tell her myself one of these days. I know you want to help, and I thank you for your concern. I miss her terribly." Graham sobbed. "I want you to come down and visit me in New York. I'll send you the fare. I don't want Ma coming around just yet. I need you to look after Whiskey Jack for me. I can't leave him on the street again. One of us has to be saved."

"I'll take care of the cat, and your mother, Graham. Nothing will stop me from helping you this time."

‡ ‡ ‡

GRAHAM AND POLINA moved to New York and acquired a small clinic at a hefty price. But it wasn't the arrangement that she had explained to him earlier.

"My parents did promise a clinic," she pouted when they discussed it. But her parents denied there had ever been the promise of a gift of a clinic to Polina. Instead, Graham was responsible for paying for it.

Her parents, a cold, critical pair of Estonians, came to her apartment when she and Graham arrived in New York.

Her father, Jakob Rebane, nodded curtly to Graham. His dark eyes were intense and appeared to hover on the edge of his sharp cheekbones. He asked no questions of Graham Currie, who politely offered him his hand to shake.

Eva Rebane's crusty face shed skin like light snow. She was a dyed blond whose straight hair limped down over her ears. Her piercing blue eyes scanned the mismatched newlyweds and blinked several times as though someone had thrown sand in her face.

"Polina says you are intelligent," Eva said to Graham. She raised her hand to hush Polina. "Intelligence is useless without ambition and curiosity," she said to him. "I hope you are lacking neither. New York is not a city for the spineless."

Her husband produced real estate papers, which were made out to Graham Currie only. The clinic came with an apartment attached at the back entrance.

"As you know," Eva continued, "we are offering you a great opportunity to advance your career here. We can secure you a licence to practise here without any trouble. My husband is chief of staff at the hospital. You will have a job, a roof over your head and . . ." She looked towards the silent Polina. "And Polina as a bonus. We own this building and more. We paid for it in full and you will have to pay us back for all these opportunities we've provided to you."

Graham swallowed hard and took a deep breath. "Why is it in my name only?" he asked.

"It is in your name only because you will be the master of your own worth. Polina will not make much difference in these matters. You'll see," Dr. Eva Rebane replied coldly.

Graham Currie looked around the clinic, at its dirty walls and windows, at its broken light fixtures, its crumbling paint. Willow Alexander's voice filled his head. Graham was too healthy to drop dead on the spot, but he wished he could. The contract was a ten-year mortgage. It would be ten years before he would be free.

He signed the contract, but not before they agreed in writing that the clinic and the apartment would be renovated at the Rebanes' expense. He watched the cruel, twisted mouths of Polina's parents as they signed on the dotted line. A week later, the contractors arrived and brought the premises back to life.

Her parents left abruptly with their papers in hand, their daughter's care now the responsibility of someone else. Henceforth, it was Graham's job to attend to her many needs. Her parents were relieved they would no longer be burdened by a child they had never planned for, a dark, deranged cargo they avoided and ignored as much as possible.

Graham Currie wondered how he would ever be able to explain this mess to Willow. She'd laugh in his face at his stupidity.

Throughout the marriage, Graham kept his head in his books and his studies. On his days off work, he took long strolls alone on a deserted beach. He wept for the clean mountain air and nature of Glenmor, longing to return home. His beloved Willow would never love or trust him again. How could she, after what he had done?

His marriage to Polina lasted the full ten dreary years. He thought of it as a jail sentence. His time alone, which was abundant—whenever she was a patient in the hospital—allowed him to specialize in internal medicine. He stayed in New York long enough for their divorce to be finalized. Polina had pleaded with him to stay in their marriage.

"I believe you are in a deep depression, my darling," she said. "My friend specializes in mental disorders. He said he would see you whenever you're ready." Graham knew her friend was another patient on her floor who saw other people's futures in a deck of cards.

"I don't need your friend, Polina. I need space. And I need this divorce."

"You have problems, Graham. You're well over two hundred pounds. That's enough to put any man over the edge. You're physically and mentally a disaster. You're eating too much junk food, and you have a habit of running away from me whenever I want to make love to you. You're a pathetic emotional quitter. You were not a foreigner to sex. Do you remember that first night?"

"Nothing happened that first night, Polina. You imagined it all. I am not blaming you. I understand who you are more clearly now."

"You promised me your grandmother's wedding ring, Graham. Someone filmed our wedding in black and white."

"Polina, there was no wedding ring. There was no one filming a black-and-white wedding."

"I saw the film. I was so beautiful. My dress had silver pearls falling like teardrops to the floor. You must have seen my dress."

"It was a movie you watched, Polina, it was not real. It's time for me to go back home."

She had been in and out of the psychiatric hospital for years. He had been stuck in a situation he hated, and in a place he couldn't wait to get away from. In a few months he would have the mortgage on the clinic paid in full. He stared at Polina, seated across from him in a private room at the psychiatric hospital. He wanted out. Graham spoke with her newly appointed psychiatrist, Dr. MacDonald. He wasn't much older than Graham himself. He'd arrived from Scotland only a few weeks earlier. They had never met before.

"I'm surprised to meet you, Graham. I thought you were one of her delusions. Man, you could have saved yourself a lot of hell had you dug a little deeper before you left Nova Scotia," the doctor said after Graham told him his story. "It has taken a lot out of you, I can see that. You are aware that you are more than likely suffering from post-traumatic stress disorder. I can give you something to carry you through the divorce."

Graham Currie wiped the sweat from his brow. "I've been counting my days to get back home." Graham voice cracked. He felt as if his lungs had been supplied with fresh air. He could breathe easier now, felt a ripple ride up and down his spine when he thought of seeing Willow again. It felt as though he were coming back to life.

Dr. MacDonald continued speaking. "Polina is a genius in her own field, but unfortunately her licence had to be revoked years ago, as you are aware. Her episodes increase when she has a target to focus on. You were no exception. It's part of her illness. She blamed her patients if their surgeries didn't go well, even threatening them. She will never be a doctor again."

"I've already set in motion the divorce proceedings," Graham replied. "I've even put the clinic up for sale."

"How did you put up with this for so long? What kind of penalty did you impose on yourself, Graham?" the psychiatrist asked.

Graham swallowed hard. "She threatened to ruin my life. And now I'm terrified of facing Willow again because I feel like such a fool. I can't believe I could ever have left Willow for a day."

"Did she marry someone else?"

"No. She lives alone at the foot of the mountain in her family home. And I still love her. I always will."

"Do you fear she wants to continue to live her life in solitude?" the doctor asked.

"Yes, I do. She was always a fighter. Fearless. Yet she never once tried to contact me to give me hell. Or even to ask what happened. Willow has succumbed to silence. I worry she will never talk to me again."

"She didn't have to give you hell—you found it on your own. I'm sure she is aware of that."

"I want to return to the mountains. But I'm terrified. I bought a medical clinic there. It was always my goal to practise in Glenmor. I want to return and get my life back on track, the way that I had planned."

"I'm sure she has not escaped the trauma of losing you. I would advise you not to put any pressure on her. Let her make her own decisions. Everything comes to an end or a beginning one way or another."

Graham lowered his head as the doctor continued to speak.

"Carry on from here. I know Polina will not adjust well once the divorce is finalized. I will keep a close eye on her. You were just what her parents wanted: someone who would be responsible for her. She'll be in and out of hospital for the rest of her life. And you have to be where you want and need to be at this point in your life."

Graham shook hands with Dr. MacDonald and thanked him for his advice.

That afternoon, Graham walked back to his clinic on the rain-swept sidewalks. He stopped for a moment and watched two pigeons fight over a mouldy crust of pizza before another slipped into the quarrel and flew off with the crust.

Graham felt an air of repentance as he watched the two pigeons pecking for loose crumbs on the wet cement. Passersby ignored him as he stood in the middle of the sidewalk. He thought about his impending freedom. The clinic would sell for a hefty price. His divorce would soon be granted. He would get his freedom, and he felt relieved.

‡ ‡ ‡

AFTER THE DIVORCE, Graham headed home to Nova Scotia under a full moon, with a duffle bag full of new clothes. In the car mirror he blinked at the decline of his own image. His receding hairline had reached the middle of his skull. Bangs like the broken teeth in a comb clung to his forehead. He looked like Friar Tuck wedged behind the wheel of a new 1985 Chevy Impala. The clinic in Glenmor would soon be ready for him to move into. One of his cousins would handle the office duties. He would live in the upstairs apartment until he built a home. As he drove, his eyes grew heavy. He pulled into a roadside motel and slept for twelve hours. In his dream, Willow Alexander lay beside him in a fetal position, refusing to speak to him.

He was on the road early and the highway was his. A little empty, a little wet, a little daring, he drove faster than usual. It was a long drive, and he had time to think things through as he drove along. His last visit to Glenmor had been after Rhona Alexander passed away.

He had not seen Willow anywhere. He drove past the house and down along the sea, but he saw nothing of the woman he had been pining for over the years. His friends filled him in on how Willow was coping after her loss. She spoke very few words to them, and asked no questions as to how he was doing in New York.

It was her eyes, they said, that caught their attention. They looked like two blank circles. Her hair fell down over her face like a wild red shield against the wind or the world. Nobody questioned her. Some people believed her vast amount of money protected her as well.

Graham was glad now that he had not spotted her. What would he have done with only a glimpse of Willow behind her shield?

The community of Glenmor knew where he had gone and what he had done in the years since he'd jilted Willow. Married a doctor, they said—he's been working in the US for years. They probably already knew he was divorced and coming home to take over Dr. Millhouse's clinic. And if they didn't, they would soon enough. Especially now that Dr. Millhouse and his wife had died so suddenly. He'd planned to come home to Glenmor, but not under such dreadful circumstances. What if the people of his hometown refused to accept him as their doctor? They had been kind to him when he came home on short visits. He never brought Polina with him. Mrs. Currie and her daughters bragged about Graham's doctor wife, but they had met her only once before she and Graham left for New York. They'd met in Halifax and got their fix on Polina. He was sure the community would make comments about his appearance behind his back. He used to be slim. Dark, curly hair. Deep and intense eyes. Now look at him.

The miles flew by under the shiny wheels of the new Impala. Graham kept himself upright with his thoughts. What kind of shape would Willow be in? His younger sister said she was as beautiful as ever but kept to herself since her parents died. Could he really blame her? What had become of both of them? What was in their future? Polina's doctor was right: Willow Alexander could not possibly have escaped the trauma when it slid in like a bolt and closed down her life. And what had it left behind? Her family were gone. Kathleen and James were deceased. Graham had disappeared. People watched Willow Alexander carefully after the Millhouses died so suddenly. They watched for the one seam that would unravel her world. They felt so sorry for the young woman whose world seemed to be cursed by tragedy. But Willow Alexander was watching and waiting. She saved her stories for the right people.

CHAPTER TWENTY-TWO

==

Lost Children

AFTER THE DEATHS OF JAMES AND KATHLEEN
Millhouse, Willow asked Mrs. Welsh if she would
sleep over during the nights. "You don't have to
stay around all day. I just want to have someone around
for the night."

Mrs. Welsh gladly accepted the offer and the extra
money it brought. She slept in the spare room upstairs,
and on the first night she heard Willow wandering
through the early hours, opening and closing cupboard
doors. Willow threw out all the jars containing powders
and spices. When Mrs. Welsh asked her why, she answered
in a low voice:

"They are of no use to me anymore."

Mrs. Welsh knew why Willow had become withdrawn
and sad. She knew what death did to people. First Willow's
father, then her mother, and now Dr. Millhouse and his

wife. They had all gone so suddenly. Mrs. Welsh's own father didn't cope well after his wife died.

"Stayed in his room naked for months," she told Willow. "My brothers were near foolish trying to talk to and feed a naked man. Finally, one morning he came down to breakfast fully dressed. Said in a dream my mother spoke to him and claimed he didn't have much to display and he should put his clothes back on. We never had an ounce of trouble with him after that."

Mrs. Welsh had to go to Halifax for a doctor's appointment and she was worried about leaving Willow on her own for a day, especially since it would be Willow's birthday. But Willow surprised her. She said it was important that Mrs. Welsh go and have things checked out, and she paid her in full for her care. Willow was thankful for the time to be alone.

‡ ‡ ‡

IN THE NEW peace and solitude of her home, Willow reflects on the last couple of weeks. She is aware how Mrs. Welsh has been watching her, probably praying that she won't have to deal with Willow holed up in her room, naked and foolish like her father. Willow knows Mrs. Welsh will understand the whole picture when she comes back from Halifax. The photos will be gone from the side table. They will be in a trunk with Mrs. Welsh's name on it. And Henry will be wrapped securely, instructions written out on notepaper so

Mrs. Welsh will know what to do with Willow's few precious belongings. She will believe Willow went totally foolish there on her own. She will have one of her sons read the note for her. The painting *Silk Kites at Dawn* will be removed from above the fireplace. Willow imagines that Mrs. Welsh will return to find smudges of soot all over the walls, the chairs, the floors, and Willow missing from the Alexander home because she has been charged with murder.

‡ ‡ ‡

WILLOW HAS FINISHED packing up her belongings and now sits against the wall in the parlour, her rubber boots beside her. *Silk Kites at Dawn* sits at her side, tightly wrapped in a blue towel. Where did the rain come from that is pelting the parlour windows like fists demanding to get in? It was sunny when she returned from her father's workshop. She feels a soft ache start inside her foot and float upwards. She listens to the silence around her and forgets for a moment what day it is.

She recalls Kathleen Millhouse's face on the morning she found their bodies, her dead smile. Then she remembers Kathleen Millhouse a week or so before her death, remembers exactly where she sat and what she was wearing.

Kathleen was always direct and full of pleasantries, nothing like her husband, who was always very formal and even referred to his wife as Mrs. Millhouse. Willow found this rather cold, as though his wife were a patient he

cared for after hours. He knew how much Willow admired
Kathleen's spirit, her quick laughter, her sharp mind. Willow
had never heard James Millhouse laugh, and his smiles were
scarce. He had a very different personality from his wife.
They couldn't have been more dissimilar.

"Opposites attract," Kathleen declared with a smile during one of Willow's tea visits. Kathleen could still walk with
a cane then. "James and I are like night and day. He is my
day and I am his night."

Willow smiled as Kathleen's words collided with her
laughter. She could not imagine them as a couple, as lovers
even. Kathleen intuited Willow's thoughts. Her voice turned
professional.

"It isn't what you imagine, young lady. We have a special relationship."

Willow picked up the empty china cups and accident-
ally dropped one into the laundry basket near the dresser,
a Royal Doulton with dainty vines crawling along the handle. It survived the fall. "Oh God," thought Willow, "please
don't let her tell me about their sex life."

"In a special relationship, people reach deeply for the
secret passages in each other." Kathleen's voice was barely
a whisper. Fatigue masked her face.

Willow coughed. How did Kathleen get past the smell
of iodine, the wiry moustache, the beard? Her face reddened with guilt. Here she stood, in their bedroom, the
most intimate space in their lives, being repulsed by a man
she didn't really know. And poor Kathleen, her face ashen

against the pillow, trying to explain her heart's desire. Willow pulled the sheet up over Kathleen before leaving the room. She had fallen asleep.

There was another important conversation with Kathleen that Willow remembers. Kathleen was sitting in her wheelchair. Willow remembers that it was so good to see her upright. There was an air of dignity in her straight posture. Kathleen held her shoulders back, her head high. Willow admired the stamina she must have called up to make herself so presentable. The beauty of her inner strength mingled with her calm expression. She wore a white cotton blouse and tan shorts. Her face was a pale palette of worn beauty, her eyes mystical as Willow placed the tray across the arms of her wheelchair. She looked strong enough to sit there all day.

"I'm happy to see you, Willow. You inspire conversations in me that I don't get from anyone else. James is not much on women's insights."

Willow smiled at her as she poured tea and placed a date square within reach.

"Pull up a chair and sit awhile!"

"I've left Dr. Millhouse's lunch on the counter. He's gone on a house call."

"Yes. He dropped in to tell me. His next patient isn't until two. We have lots of time to talk."

This made Willow a bit uneasy. Kathleen had that professional look in her eyes. She was always so direct.

"James tells me you have a lovely home at the foot of the mountain."

"It was my father's family home. He never left it. My mother sold her home when they married."

"Is that why you've never left it?"

Willow could feel the sweat collecting in her palm. "Don't drop another cup," she thought. She didn't answer the question. It was more complicated than a yes-or-no answer. And Willow wasn't ready to discuss the long answer.

"Your father performed a very noble deed. All of his siblings were very well-educated, I've been told."

"He didn't have much choice. His mother wasn't able to do it. He exchanged his own goals for theirs."

"Is that why you resent them? I've noticed you always refer to them as 'my father's sisters' and 'my father's brothers.' You have detached from any relationship with them."

Willow was taken aback by these words. She had never spoken them aloud to herself, but she knew it was true. She did detach her aunts and uncles from herself.

"I resent the fact that he was robbed of his own childhood, and he had to listen to their success stories when they came to visit."

"His mother and siblings had no control over the situation," Kathleen said softly. "Death doesn't come with instructions, only solutions, Willow. There's no doubt they see him as a great and loving man."

Willow got up and paced the floor. Her head ached with this very personal discussion.

"Sit down, Willow. You can tell me to mind my own business at any time. But you won't, because you know the truth when you hear it. You're very bright. Yet you stayed on the mountain too. Could you be disappointed by your own goals? What were you looking forward to?"

Willow moved quietly back to the chair. "I just knew all my dreams and goals were beside this mountain. Graham's clinic and my work as his assistant was what I wanted most. A person can see the world in between. I wanted my father's contentment."

"That's a noble cause, Willow, but I'm sure you know what can happen to the best-laid plans of mice and men."

"I know that the men marry other woman, Kathleen. I don't know what the mice do." She laughed in relief.

"Did you ever wonder what would have happened to your father's brothers and sisters if they'd been separated? Your grandmother was lucky she could stay at home. They took great care of her, the family and friends. Your father was a hero to them. No amount of formal education could compete with his achievements. He was a hero to my husband, an inspiration. He admired your father greatly. He said your father was a rare breed of a man."

Willow nodded her head in agreement. Kathleen poured herself a second cup of tea. Her hand was a bit shaky. Willow reached for the teapot, but Kathleen looked at Willow and laughed.

"You didn't think I could do it, did you?"

"No, not really."

"I wanted to prove something to you. Perseverance is useful."

"It reminds me of when I was a child in the principal's office."

"What were you called to the principal's office for?" Kathleen asked with a grin.

"Marjorie, my best friend, was accused of cheating on a test when we were ten. I knew she didn't do it. Someone threw a piece of paper on her desk with an answer written on it. The teacher found it and sent her to the office to get the strap. I told the teacher she didn't do it, so I got sent down to the principal's office with her."

"What happened?"

"We both got the strap. But I refused to cry, so the principal hit me harder and I just stood there and smiled at him."

After all these years, Willow still closed her fists to smother the stings from the strap. She remembered the principal's face was in a purple rage, looking down at her deliberate smile, her act of defiance. She remembered Marjorie's sobs, and how the tremble in her right hand was comforted by the left that had yet to be punished.

Kathleen's voice broke into her memories. "Good for you. You taught yourself a lesson," she said. "When circumstances get out of your control, you either give in or take the high road. I'm sure your father felt like crying many times. But his determination and perseverance turned him into the man he became."

"My father was much stronger than I'll ever be. I used to believe my mother was meek and naive until the day he died. That was the day she stayed at his side. I wouldn't go into the room until I heard her cry out, until I knew it was all over. She was holding his dead body in her arms. I miss them most when the darkness crawls in and mingles with silence in the house." Willow gulped down the tea. Her throat felt dry and stiff.

"You're more like your father than you realize, Willow," Kathleen said. "I know how hard their passing must be for you to deal with at times. I must tell you that my home life was much different than yours. My parents were alcoholics. I was raised by my aunt in another city. My younger siblings were adopted out. I never saw them again."

Willow could hear the pounding in her chest. She couldn't look at Kathleen, as she thought of the hidden and terrible things in her body that would soon rear their ugly heads and take her life.

"Willow, look at me," Kathleen said, her voice soft like a splash of warm water. "I want you to see things for what they are. Death will come to all of us. I've lived. I've loved. What more do I need?"

Willow finally stood up. "I don't know how to feel. Marjorie moved away when we were teenagers. Graham left when I was twenty-four. I miscarried a month later. I took a trip to Rome. I took a medical secretary's course—I believed it would come in handy when Graham returned. My parents died. And now I am forty years old and alone. I know I stayed on the mountain because I knew my father wouldn't reach old age. And I knew my mother would need me, and I couldn't leave her alone."

Willow stands like a glass figurine as she remembers her conversation with Kathleen. Intelligent people like Kathleen miss nothing. She could see right through Willow. After speaking with Kathleen, Willow felt as though her whole being had been emptied.

A stiff breeze had been playing in the white drapes that day. The gentle force wafted in towards a small desk, then slammed like a wave against rocks. Two photos crashed to the floor. Her mother would have believed a ghost had entered the room.

Willow had never before mentioned to anyone that she had lost a baby, not even her best friend Marjorie. The thought of mentioning it to Marjorie made it too real. Yet she saw nothing but empathy in Kathleen's eyes, a secret sorrow only a woman could connect with, an emptiness that reached far beyond the room and looked directly into an empty crib.

Willow closed the balcony door and picked up the shattered photos. One photo was a small girl of two or three, wrapped in frills and lace to the tips of her white shoes. Her small hands cradled a little book. The ears of a rabbit were clearly visible on the cover. The child had a distant look in her eyes, as though someone had requested that she close the book at the best part of the story. Or perhaps the story had ended, and the child wanted to hear it from the beginning again.

Willow would have read from books like this to her own

child, had the baby lived. A plump little brown rabbit had crossed her path the evening she went up the mountain to bury her lost child. It stopped, then scurried under a tree. She was carrying one of the wooden canisters her father had carved for her as a wedding gift. She had placed a warm blanket around the remains of her baby and put it into a bag. It was the canister that said *Sugar*. At the time, Willow thought this was appropriate, something to sweeten her grief. She had slipped out and up the side of the mountain when her parents left the house. From the bathroom floor, she'd scraped a handful of bloody cloths and placed them in the sugar canister and flushed the remainder down the toilet. She took a small shovel from beside the shed with her.

Her body ached. Her parents were at the community hall preparing for a reception that night, an anniversary party for a couple whose marriage had lasted sixty years. She knew she would have to dig deep enough to keep the animals from picking up the scent of blood. The first turning of the sod was back-breaking, and she sat against the trunk of the sturdy maple afterwards and took deep breaths. Eventually, there was a safe depth in the ground, and she placed the sugar canister of bloody cloths into a tobacco can to keep the scent of blood from the animals— and placed her child slowly into the earth.

Willow couldn't remember getting back home, back to her bed, where she saw the ceiling floating like a black cloud above her head and falling towards her. She woke up several hours later. It was dark. The house was quiet. Her parents must have left for the reception. They knew that Willow wouldn't attend anything at the hall. She kept to her room these days. In a few days she would check the small grave again, and no one would ever know. The only witness was the plump brown rabbit.

Her parents died without ever knowing what she'd buried on the side of the mountain. She knew her child would have been loved. Her mother might have said, "The dear child should know its father. I never knew mine. For years I believed he was a ghost. Don't introduce your child to a ghost, Willow!"

Returning to the present, she was aware that Kathleen hadn't taken her eyes off her. She'd watched Willow cradle the picture of the small child with such care and stroke the child's face. Willow didn't ask the child's name. The answer would disturb her.

"I doubt if I will ever marry," Willow said to Kathleen. "I would've understood if Graham had said he wanted to wait until he was finished med school to get married."

Kathleen looked kindly at Willow. "It was immature of him to do what he did. He had his studies to contend with and great career advancement in the States, a new world to explore. He was young. But that's no excuse for his behaviour. I believe he is full of self-doubt to this day. His emotional world is empty, and he has no idea how to fill it. That doesn't make him a bad person. People do harmful things to each other and to themselves. Did you ever ask yourself why you kept your own secret?"

Willow listened to the sound of her own heartbeat, to the secret that lay behind its loud tapping. "Fear," she whispered as she looked directly into the eyes of her dying friend. "He always believed I was fearless, but in this case my heart worked faster than my mouth."

Willow could hear the beginning rasp of fatigue in Kathleen's voice. "Well, perhaps we can talk about it some more tomorrow. I'll let you get back to work."

Willow caught Kathleen's hidden intention. Her friend had led her down a path she had refused to travel until now.

Kathleen was in ill health for the next two weeks. Willow did not bring her tea. Irene gave her updates. Dr. Millhouse kept his head down. Willow asked him no personal questions.

"Give Kathleen my best," Willow said to him on her way home from work one Friday.

He looked up at her without expression. "Did you ever see a doctor after your miscarriage?" he asked. "It can lead to infections and other uterine problems."

Willow's feet turned to cement. She was moving and yet seemed to stand still. "Who told you about my miscarriage? The only person I ever told was Kathleen."

"What is said to Mrs. Millhouse stays with Mrs. Millhouse," he said.

"Then who told you?"

"Nobody, Willow. I've been dealing with such matters for years. A woman never loses that maternal image in her eyes. I see how you reach out to babies and children who come to the office. If all is well, you could still have a child."

Willow's mind wandered to random thoughts—babies' names, the first taste of ice cream, the beginning of school, tin cans and Kathleen Millhouse. There was no way Kathleen would have mentioned their private conversation. She knew how difficult it was for Willow to talk about her personal life.

Willow left the office that day and walked home, still thinking about her child. She imagined a red mass of hair, a pair of green eyes widening on Christmas morning, a small hand waving from the window of a school bus. A trip up the mountain with his mother. Her precious son calling out to the rabbits. She was so sure her child would have been a boy. He would have been the gift his father left behind for her.

The following week, Willow made a visit to Kathleen after she asked to see her. Willow was dressed in blue. She watched Kathleen's eyes follow a palette trail from Willow's dark-blue sweater to the lighter-blue dress and the pale-blue ribbon holding her hair back from her face. The eyes of the dying take in the whole person in front of them.

"I used to wear ribbons in my hair, Willow," Kathleen said. "In fact, I was wearing one when James asked me to marry him."

"They come in handy when you keep your head down at your desk," Willow replied.

"How handy are they when you keep your head up?"

"I've never given it much thought, Kathleen."

"Please sit down, Willow, while I still have a bit of wind left in my lungs."

"Are you in pain?"

"Pain is a mysterious entity. That's why most people have a hard time figuring out where it all started. I can handle physical pain, Willow, just like you do."

Willow had never measured pain in any one category. She had grey areas when it came to relatives, teachers, classmates and strangers. Internal, emotional pain came and stayed when Marjorie's family left, and when her unborn child was washed from her womb like a savage current. And, of course, when Graham vanished. Thinking about her parents also gave her pain. At times she believed her parents were still here, hanging around like paintings. She placed them in patches of familiar scenes in the fields. The swift strides her father made with his scythe in the tall hay. The opening and closing of the screen door when he entered or left. The gentle tapping of footwear he made on the step. Her mother, a delicate beauty, spent hours in the pantry lining up jars of preserved fruit, her sacred orchard at the end of her fingertips. Her father in the workshop while Willow sat in the rocker. The soft rhythm the rocking made on the wood floor as he worked, and the charm of his handsomeness whenever he winked over at her.

Kathleen stared at her with a smile on her face. "We've known each other for a few years now. It doesn't take long for minds to connect when they have shared the same sorrow."

Willow looked down at her. She looked cold; a defrost-
ing stream of sweat ran down the side of her nose. She was
still a pretty woman, with large, misty eyes, who was sinking back into a shrinking face the size of a child's. Her pale
lips traced her words with her tongue before she released
them. It was her mind, the razor blade of her strength, that
kept her talking.

"Speak often of those you've loved and lost. I saw your
affection for the child in the photo. You will find it again.
You will love again. The child in the photo died when . . ."

Kathleen drifted off just as Willow knelt close to better hear her story. Willow then walked quietly over to the
dresser and picked up the picture of the child again. There
was no name or date written on the back of the photo. The
child remained a mystery. Was she Kathleen's child? Willow
decided she would not mention the child to Kathleen again.

CHAPTER TWENTY-THREE

—

A Paper-Thin Divide

KATHLEEN'S VOICE COMES BACK TO HER THROUGH the wind of an open window. "Speak often of those you've loved and lost."

How appropriate for Willow and Graham. The leftovers of Christy's Mountain, who had made love for the first time at seventeen under a maple tree. Willow had shaped a bed from the earth from moss. There was no one to stop them. Nobody. Willow had told her mother they were going to pick berries. She had even given them a bucket.

There is a paper-thin divide between love and hate. The idea of Graham's return both excites and angers Willow. She has known him all her life, and yet she never really knew him until he disappeared fifteen years ago. Maybe her mother was not mistaken when she said the man she had seen in the graveyard that stormy day looked familiar to her.

"I wasn't afraid of him," Rhona said.

Did Graham go to the graveyard, if it was really him, to see if he might meet her at her father's gravesite? A proper place for a condolence, a reunion, and yet had he ignored her distraught mother that night she'd been caught in a raging storm? If he had driven her mother home, offered his formal condolences and made his appearance known, would it have shed a different light on the man Willow once believed she knew? She might never know if her mother saw anyone at all.

Willow realizes now that there is one secret she will no longer keep from Graham Currie: their unborn child. She will not renege on what she believes her mother would have wanted. No more ghosts in this family.

She wonders what kind of reception Graham expects from her. She already knows he bought Dr. Millhouse's clinic. He will be less than a mile from her door. "I am returning alone," he wrote in his letter to her, an open acknowledgement of his marital freedom.

Willow wonders what it all means. What does he really see in his future? Does it include a single woman who never left the mountain? Another woman with medical training and money to burn? She wishes she'd had more time with Kathleen to ask her advice.

Willow hears the phone ringing in the parlour. Four, five, six rings before she crawls up off the floor and reaches for it with a sooty hand. Marjorie's mother's voice is warm and inviting.

"Willow, how are you, dear?"

There is a long pause before Willow clears her throat. "How are you, Alma?"

"I'm not calling about myself. I want to know about you. I heard the terrible news about Dr. Millhouse and his wife."

There is something Willow wants to say, words she wants to share with the woman who lined her children up and pretended she would cart them off to jail for innocent childhood scuffles. Perhaps Alma will scoop her into her massive arms and smother her in love. Willow knows Alma is one of the few people she can turn to now.

"Are you still there, Willow?"

"Yes, I'm here."

"I'm coming to Glenmor next week, dear," Alma tells her. "Will you be okay until then?"

"Yes. Thank you, Alma. I'm fine. I'll see you next week." Willow hangs up the phone and looks around the parlour. A map of soot surrounds her, a black trail testifying to what has taken place, the removal of things she's erased from her life in anticipation of her arrest.

She thinks of the wedding photos of her relatives that she has packed away. Her grandmother, Edith, who had the widest smile. Who knows why? Bella, the one who dined on black tea for a week before going to her black grave, was the most beautiful. And the photo of her mother, Rhona, in the damp field with her bouquet of daises. Willow has no wedding photos of herself, although she remembers someone snapping a picture of her as she walked up the long steps towards the double doors. The edge of her train was wrapped around her left arm. Perhaps that Kodak moment is in someone's album. "Spinster in a Wedding Dress," they would call the photo. She doesn't know who took it.

Willow wonders what would have happened on her wedding night had there been one. She was already pregnant. The news was going to be her wedding gift to Graham. She had been carrying his baby behind her wildflowers. How would Graham have taken this news? They had talked about having children someday. Two, he said, company for one another. A son was what Willow had hoped for first. Graham had been surrounded by too much female persuasion all his life. She'd always wanted a large family, four children at least.

Suddenly, Willow is not sure of anything. The emptiness feels overwhelming. The blue sky is hidden somewhere out of reach. The sun is lying low, waiting for an opening. And the wind is as breathless as a sniper hiding in the trees. The weather is threatening. Willow has no desire to start the fire and make a cup of tea. What is above her roof and beyond her windows will have to settle in its own course.

All she can think is that Graham Currie is coming back home. Home from a prison she knows nothing about, while she had entered a prison of her own that he knows nothing about. Something crosses her mind. They will meet again soon. But where?

Mrs. Welsh calls to check on her. "I'll be staying with my sister for a week or so. A battery of tests, they say, before they'll peel the cataract from my eye. You'd think it was a banana that was blurring my sight."

"Alma is coming for a visit next week," answers Willow. "You take whatever time you need." Willow speaks slowly, distracted by the happy thought of having the place to herself for a while.

How will she explain things to her beloved Alma, who is on her way because she knows by instinct that there is something brewing that Willow will not be able to handle on her own? Alma knows she can get Willow to let go of whatever is pulling her down. Alma is good at doing those kinds of things for people.

A bouncing pain begins to play havoc in Willow's spine, starting and stopping between her shoulder blades and running like crippled notes down her back. She crawls up on one knee and pulls herself up. Once on her feet, she leans against the wall for support. She runs her hands over her mother's painting *Silk Kites at Dawn* and smiles faintly at thirty-five years of memories. The silk moon and stars depict a pivotal moment of her childhood. She is not sure what will become of the painting if she is arrested for the Millhouses' deaths. She will offer it to Marjorie. She knows Marjorie would love to hang the painting in her home when

she moves back to the mountain with her family. There is
something else that she can do for Marjorie and her family:
she will offer her home to them until she returns, if all goes
against her. Why has she been so troubled over what will
happen to her possessions when there is someone else to
love them for her while she is away?

A squint of sunlight appears in the eastern window. The
trees on the mountain are still shedding steady drops from
their branches. Willow moves closer to the window. She's
always loved the scent and beauty of mountain rain.

Willow hears a woodpecker in the distance. She's never
been fond of these early risers. Her father had to repair
his barn roof more than once because of their destructive
pecking. But her father always forgave the woodpeckers.

"They're just doing what nature intended," he'd say,
smiling.

Willow taps her nail on the windowpane.

Tap. Tap. Tap.

Is Graham returning to roost in Glenmor?

Tap. Tap.

══

CHAPTER TWENTY-FOUR

A Deep Hunger

GRAHAM HAD ALWAYS HAD A COMPLICATED RELA-
tionship with the truth. He generally avoided it.
The closer he got to home, the more his stress
escalated. He stopped for lunch at a fast-food takeout and
ate three hamburgers and two milkshakes.

His pulse raced. Questions remained unanswered in his
head. "Should I drive up to Willow's door and tell her what
really happened?" Not likely. She probably wouldn't believe
him. Why would she, after all these years? He would never
be that brave anyway.

"You didn't steal her last stick of gum and hide it in your
jeans!" he blurted out to himself, angry at his own lack of
understanding.

No. I shattered her trust. Robbed her of her wedding
day. Made her wait in front of everyone for me to show
up. Candles don't burn forever; they eventually go out. He

imagines the scene, after he left her at the altar. Spirals of smoke rising behind her while the village watched her drive away. The off-white Spinster Bride, and the maid of honour beside her, in blue. Her mother, head bowed. Her father, stoic as always, as if it was not a surprise to him. He knew love is a cold emotion in the seams of the weak, and it's sometimes fatal for those who try to crawl back in to warm it up. Willow might not want to see him again.

She would know that he was back, though. Mrs. Welsh would be the one to let her know if the village had welcomed him back or not. He would have to make the initial visit. It would be too awkward to meet her in public. He wondered if he should phone first, ask if he could come to the house. He was anxious to see her and talk to her in person, something he should have done before now. What would he have done if she had left *him* standing in the church? And now, so many years later, he was returning, divorced, overweight, balding, and wanting a new beginning. How would he explain his vanished years to her? That in all those years he had felt as if he were in a prison. She was no fool.

Hours later, he pulled into a roadside diner and ordered a hot turkey sandwich with extra gravy.

"The coffee is lukewarm," he said to the tired waitress. "And the gravy is the same."

"The world is lukewarm, mister," she replied. "I'm brewing a fresh pot of coffee, but that's the last of the gravy. I can't warm it up cuz the microwave's broke."

Graham noticed the bulging veins in her heavy legs and the swelling in her ankles. He wanted to ask her what her doctor prescribed for her condition, but he didn't. She was well aware of her own misery. Why should he bring it to her attention when she already knew? Her face was a billboard of agony. This was one worry he could lay to rest about Willow. She had a good job and a home. He couldn't imagine her serving lukewarm coffee in a roadside diner.

His meeting with the Millhouses had been unexpected. He had received a phone call from his sister saying that Dr. Millhouse was interested in speaking with him. Graham met with him a couple of weeks later. He knew Kathleen Millhouse's condition was grave when he saw her then. She was a psychologist; he'd read her work in medical school. James Millhouse himself was a genius, an ace of a diagnostician who was widely respected. His name was well-known in medical circles. Graham could understand why Glenmor would be appealing to them. Kathleen needed the slow pace, the clean air. But they needed to go, and the sale of the clinic was wrapped up in a week. And now they were gone. He had some concerns about stepping in. He knew most of the people who would come under his care, and they would be his harshest critics.

He finished the turkey and coffee. He pulled a fifty-dollar bill from his wallet and told the waitress to keep the change. Behind the wheel, he revved up the engine and backed out of his parking spot. He heard a scattering of small pebbles hit the Impala as he shot out onto the highway. He had a deep hunger to get back to work. He thought of the waitress at the diner again. The poor woman should not have been on her feet with her legs in that condition. She no doubt had no choice. He did have a choice in his life, though. He should have returned to Glenmor after he graduated. But he chose another road. A dark one.

But now that he had his freedom back again, he had new choices to make.

CHAPTER TWENTY-FIVE

==

Set Free

WILLOW DOESN'T HEAR THE VEHICLE WHEN IT pulls up to her house. She hears only the banging on her back door. She grips the chair to raise herself off the floor and quickly pulls on her old track suit and rubber boots. Had she fallen asleep? She doesn't remember. The rain has stopped, the sun blazes through the window. She reaches to the floor and picks up the painting of *Silk Kites at Dawn*, then opens the door to two Mounted Police officers standing on her doorstep.

Willow steps outside onto the porch to face the officers. The spring rains have nourished her mother's gardens. The tulips dance in aggressive splendour, oblivious to the still-lingering cool breezes of May. Their roots are well fed in the womb of Mother Earth. The police officers, one male and one female, say good morning and introduce themselves. Willow recognizes them from Dr. Millhouse's office, and she is aware that they recognize her. The introductions are simply a formality, she suspects, in their line of work.

The female officer's eyes survey the gardens. She draws her fingers over the petals of the tulips along the step. It's obvious she prefers the red ones. The male officer holds a brown folder in his hand. They both size up Willow's appearance. Their eyes trace the black soot on her hands and face and the smudges on the cloth that conceals the painting in her hand.

The woman officer speaks in a soft voice. "Are you Willow Alexander?"

"Yes," Willow answers.

The male officer checks his folder before he speaks. "I'm sure you're aware why we're here."

"Awareness can be a contemptuous vice, officer," Willow says. "I've been waiting for you."

"We have a few questions we would like to ask you down at the police station concerning the Millhouses. I know you knew them on a personal level more than anyone else in Glenmor."

"Yes," Willow confirms. "I worked for him for several years."

"We would like to talk to you before we wrap up the case."

The policewoman speaks slowly to Willow, as if to a child. "Would you like a few minutes . . . to wash up before we go?"

Willow's voice is direct. "I don't need to wash up. My answers will be the same whether I'm dirty or clean." Then abruptly she asks, "How long does it take for the officials to complete an autopsy?"

"We were trying to trace family members, but there don't appear to be any." His voice is professional. "The family is the first to get the results of the autopsies."

The female officer stands face to face with Willow. "We wonder if you are aware of any family members." She has her arm around Willow's shoulder. "Can you come down to the station with us?"

Willow sits down on the damp step. She can feel a numbness crawling up her legs. There are no relatives for them to locate for Kathleen. And she knows of no family for James either. She cannot recall who maintained the old Millhouse family home, or if they ever told her who occupied it now.

The two officers help her up by the arms and walk her to the back door of the cruiser.

"Is there anything you'd like to do before we leave?"

"Yes, sir. I would like to feed my pet crow. I forgot to give him his treat yesterday."

Willow calls out his name. The crow doesn't appear, so she leaves the food on the gatepost.

The female officer opens the car door and helps her gently into the back seat. Willow can hear muffled whispers between the officers.

"What does she have in that cloth?"

"God knows."

Willow smiles. How could they understand that Kathleen Millhouse was connected to this painting by a ribbon of blue silk?

Willow rolls down the back window of the cruiser. The officer turns the key in the ignition.

"Stop. Listen, listen!" Willow cries out.

They can hear Sorrow calling, "Willooooo," as the cruiser rolls slowly down the lane.

As they drive towards the police station, they pass the medical clinic. Willow is surprised to see so many workers and all the changes that have already been made to the building. A wooden sign—carved with black-and-gold lettering—is being hung above the main entrance. Willow's father made the sign, at Willow's request, when she and Graham graduated from high school: GRAHAM CURRIE M.D., it reads. Willow always liked to get a jump on things. Willow notices that the door on the balcony leading to the Millhouses' bedroom is opened wide.

When they arrive at the door of the police station, the female officer escorts Willow to a small office inside. The officer leaves the room for a few minutes, then returns with a glass of cold water and a warm cloth.

"For your hands," she says, passing Willow the cloth. Willow wipes off her hands and rolls the cloth into a ball. The male officer comes in and sits at the desk.

"Are you feeling better, Miss Alexander?" he asks politely.

"I'm sorry we had to bother you, but as I said, we've been trying to locate relatives of the Millhouses."

Willow stares at the dying geranium plant in the window. The petals have fallen to the floor like drops of blood. "They need the proper light," Willow says, looking down at the fallen petals.

The officers exchange a glance before returning their attention to Willow.

"This won't take long," the male officer says. His voice has turned parental.

Willow sits upright and sips the water, feeling as though a safety net has been released.

"We need to find the relatives before we can release the remains," he explains again.

"I doubt if you'll find any living relatives," Willow says. "Dr. Millhouse's parents died when he was a small child. Kathleen was adopted by an aunt. She lost contact years ago with her siblings when they were adopted out." Willow is surprised at the sound of her own voice. It is firm and coherent. "I suggest you contact the hospital in Manitoba where Dr. Millhouse last worked. I have the name in my files. I know they did a locum at the Mayo Clinic at one point. His former friends and colleagues could be of help to you."

She notices that the officer is writing in his folder at a furious pace. A recording machine wheezes on the desk. Between it all, she can hear the officer talking to himself.

She looks directly at him. "Will you be able to release the cause of their deaths to me?"

He looks up at the other officer and back at Willow. "I'm afraid not, Miss Alexander. Why are you asking?" He adds a quick note in his folder.

Willow takes a deep breath before answering. "I've been waiting for the last few weeks to be arrested. I believe I may have mistakenly put rodent poison in the cake I brought to them the night before I found their bodies."

The officer stares at her for a moment as though she has begun to speak in Arabic. Then he understands and quickly shakes his head.

"They were not poisoned, Miss Alexander," he says. "That's not how they died."

There is a long silence before anyone speaks again. Willow tightens her grip on the glass. Even before the information is revealed to her, even before the last image of Kathleen's pale face swims up from the water in the glass and places itself close enough to reach out and touch, Willow has figured it out. James Millhouse was drinking that night. He spilled out his life in thin sentences. He had saved many lives, and yet he was dying from a disease that belonged to Kathleen. He'd suffered its side effects for years as he watched his beautiful wife's life being swept away. He had watched, helplessly, as days turned into nights, and months into years. He was unable to unlock her beautiful body and let her go free.

In that moment, Willow Alexander realizes that she is not a murderer. Dr. Millhouse decided to set both of them free of his wife's disease.

The police decide to confide in Willow, to assure her that she is not responsible for their deaths. A letter was found in Dr. Millhouse's desk drawer, along with the needles he'd used. His lethal goodbyes. His description of the eventful night is scrawled on a sheet of typing paper, and the police read it out to Willow:

My wife was barely conscious when I went to her room. Her breathing was laboured. Her blood pressure was slid-ing. I sat with her for the longest time. She is now free . . . I went back to my office and sat at my desk. Dr. Morrison phoned . . . I finished my tea . . . took a few bites of cake at her last request . . . she had a smile on her face . . . I feel free . . . I'm very . . . very tired . . . Kathleen . . . are you . . .

‡ ‡ ‡

THAT AFTERNOON, ON the drive home from the police sta-tion, Willow notices that the balcony door to the Millhouses' bedroom is now closed. She has never believed in omens or superstitions the way her mother did. Yet she feels the sting of a finale, a play she doesn't want to end. She thinks of all the events from the past fifteen years: The devastation of her father's death, followed by her mother's. Her final goodbyes with the Millhouses. Her last day with Marjorie, who sat in the old truck, heading down the mountain to the city, holding the music of her childhood in a battered fiddle case. Graham's finale, no music or farewell, just gone. And finally, the abrupt farewell of her lost baby, which hurt most of all.

==

CHAPTER TWENTY-SIX

The Man in the Impala

BACK HOME, WILLOW LOOKS AROUND THE HOUSE AT the empty spaces where the framed brides had stood on the little side table for years, where the alert, always-on-duty Henry the butler once held sway. She'd released them too early, perhaps in the same way all of those she loved had also left before their time. Now that she knows she is not going to jail, she will remove them from their trunks and dark closets and bring them back to where they belong.

She hangs the kite painting back in its spot above the fireplace. She stands back and examines it, finding intricacies she has never noticed before: The edge of her braids, the way they were wind-swept off her shoulders. Her father, down on one knee, his massive hands entwined in blue silk. But what surprises her the most—how could she have missed it all this time?—is the lone figure at the edge of the painting. The slim figure of a woman, in a long white dress, at the edge of the clearing, muted but clearly visible now to Willow.

Willow listens to the hum of the kettle before she puts the tea in the pot. She decides on a full pot of tea this morning, for no apparent reason, since she is expecting no company. She sits with her cup at the kitchen table. A monarch butterfly flutters near the edge of the window, waves and flits off to a nearby bush, its colourful beauty part of its identity, a black spot on a vein on each wing revealing that its metamorphosis into an adult is complete. Willow smiles at the beauty of it. She can hear Kathleen's voice whispering, "Don't ever give up on beauty, girl. Don't ever give up your rainbow."

‡ ‡ ‡

A WEEK AFTER Willow's visit to the police station, she learns that the Millhouses' ashes are to be forwarded to a distant cousin of Kathleen's who lives at the old homestead out west. But there is a delay because the cousin has an illness and wants to be well enough to attend their burial. In the meantime, the ashes are kept in a back room at the police station.

Willow refuses to call the Millhouses' ending a murder/suicide. It was the act of a man who was no longer capable of injecting life into his beloved wife's body. Kathleen would have expected him to keep on living. But James no longer had a reason, or so he believed.

Mrs. Welsh has told Willow many times that she married her husband, Clovis, not out of love but out of pity. He lost an eye in an accident, had kidney problems and couldn't hear more than three words out of ten on any given day.

"Clovis had a beautiful heart," Mrs. Welsh told Willow one day at the kitchen table. "He was kind to everyone. Good as gold to our boys." She said the local girls refused to dance with him because he couldn't hear the music. "He would be waltzing when everyone else would be going full swing at the polka!"

"You were very kind to him," Willow said, observing the leftover love in Mrs. Welsh's eyes for her departed Clovis, the obedience that reflects the art of true love. Mrs. Welsh stopped and listened to what her husband couldn't hear and described whole images to him that he was not able to see. At the end of each day was their special hour. She would place the rose-coloured teapot between the two cups and put out the oatcakes fresh from the afternoon oven, as well as a stack of books whose words Mrs. Welsh had never learned to read but whose stories came to life for her through her husband's voice.

Willow didn't hear the exchange between her parents when her father died. She stayed in the parlour as her mother fed him his last meal. Willow remembers watching the coming dusk in Glenmor that evening as it came tearing through the fog. The mountain creaked and settled. Rabbits dined under trees. The owls watched and waited. Then nature turned up a gust of wind that knocked a photo off the side table. Willow watched it fall. Rhona and Murdoch Alexander. She bent forward and picked it up. That's when Willow heard her father's name come bouncing down the hall, off the walls, her mother's sharp and piercing cry like a spray of bullets. Willow then walked slowly down the hall as though being pulled by a rope towards her mother's haunting sobs.

There are no more voices in the Alexander home, and Willow is free in the silence. She is beginning to feel that the knots that tied back her life have finally loosened. Alma is expected to arrive soon, so Willow washes the walls and the floors, then refills the cupboards with fresh spices and flour.

"Don't fuss for me, dear!" Alma had said before hanging up.

Willow makes a lemon pie, a chocolate cake and a pot of fish chowder. She thanks her mother under her breath for the domestic abilities she passed on to her. As Willow expected, Alma arrives with armfuls of love. Willow sits at the table and relaxes as Alma serves up the fish chowder between peals of laughter.

"Child, your bones are capable of carrying another twenty pounds," she pronounces as only a mother could. "Look at me, Willow. I've carted this flesh around for years. If I lost it now, I'd be frantic wondering where I went."

A rapid slice of laughter fills the kitchen. Alma takes pride in laughing at her own sense of self. She is wearing a bright flowered dress that hangs down over her knees like an overgrown garden. On her feet, in worn slippers, she prances gracefully from stove to table, an aging ballerina determined not to forget her steps. She sings as she works; music directs her motions.

"I love the mountains. When my man retires, we'll be back," Alma says happily.

Willow smiles at her. "I can't wait!"

They move on to the lemon pie. Alma savours each bite, glad to have a break from cooking.

"Did you know that Graham is on his way back to the mountain?" Willow asks, keeping her eyes down.

"That doesn't surprise me, Willow. I knew he'd be back someday."

"He wrote to tell me about his plans. He bought the clinic from Dr. Millhouse."

"How convenient for him. He flies off like a moth, collects some New York dust and comes back to Glenmor to sprinkle it around, like nothing happened. But there is always a fly in the ointment when people change too quickly. I suspect there is something he got caught up in . . . but it's none of my business. One should never judge a situation until it calls out your name."

"Kathleen Millhouse advised me to think things through."

Alma's smile fades. "Such a shame about those nice people. He sounds like a man who refused to collect pity. But pity collected him." Alma sighs and continues. "But when it comes to Graham Currie, all I can say, Willow, is stand your ground. You owe him nothing, and nothing should be his reward." She laughs.

Willow's smile follows. Alma wraps her in a bear hug and looks over Willow's head at the spotless emptiness that surrounds her. There is more to this story, but she feels that she has said enough for now. In Willow's eyes, a dry storm looms. Alma has never seen Willow weep, even as a child. She was always polite and stoic, with a slow release of a smile.

"Did I mention to you that Marjorie is returning to Nova Scotia too?" Alma exhales. "She asked me not to say a word until they train someone else to take over her job. She's planning to get her teaching degree. I know you can use some good news. Act surprised when she tells you!"

"She's been telling me this for quite a while now. I know she wants to have your house rebuilt."

Alma wipes the tears from her eyes. "I know. She's such a kind child. She's been saving every penny."

A few minutes later, Willow turns slightly as a shadow moves along the road. She notices a dark Impala slowing down, as if the driver is looking for something.

"Are you expecting someone, Willow?" Alma asks, noticing the car as well.

"No, not really. People slow down sometimes when they pass by the property."

"Can't say I blame them. You've kept your mother's garden like a Victorian showplace."

Willow watches as the car parks at the foot of the mountain, a few feet from the path. Her visits up the mountain are less frequent now. Habitual grief, she supposes. A man stands looking up at the mountain. He remains in front of the car, partially hidden. Willow can't make out the licence plate from this distance. One hand is held over the man's right eye, blocking out the sun.

===

CHAPTER TWENTY-SEVEN

The Secret of the Mountain

THE FIRST DAY OF GRAHAM CURRIE'S RETURN IS marked with blood.

He removes his sunglasses as he faces the mountain. He didn't plan to visit here so soon after returning to Glenmor. But one does not make plans for the mountain; the mountain makes plans for you. He has nothing to offer its graces—no beauty, no maintenance, no defiance. The mountain covets the dead, lures lovers into its snarled webs, and plays hide-and-seek with moonshiners who plant their stills deep in its wild flesh. In its wilderness, many a lost soul has succumbed to madness. Do not enter without your exit marked!

A flood of scrambled emotions converges in Graham's head. He despises what he has become. Here he is, at forty years of age, chasing down the hunger of bygone days. He has spoken three or four sentences before he realizes he is talking out loud. To whom? White spit collects in the corners of his mouth. This is the perfect spot for him to dispose of his anger. Spray it into the trees like hot piss. He knows he can't put any of this on anyone else's shoulders but his own.

He is so wrapped up in his own thoughts, he doesn't hear the sound of someone walking towards him.

Suddenly, Willow appears, beautiful and determined. They stare at each other. There is a feral look in her eyes. She wants his blood but is waiting for him to take the first bite. Someone in the background is calling out her name, but she ignores it. The calling stops.

"You're late, Graham. Ten years or more." The words came from the corner of her mouth. Her hand is dancing around it as though she is trying to pry it open to let out more pain. He has seen this look in the eyes of patients who have been told, "We couldn't get it all."

He gets a good look at her. Her voice is deeper. Her eyes are as cold as old frost. Around her head, her hair is wild. She looks like a wild animal awoken from sleep. She is clearly angry. He remains silent. What can he say in this moment? He is not prepared for a confrontation.

"Why did you come back?" She watches the hunch of his shoulders. The up-and-down sway of thick, sweating flesh rippling under his dark shirt annoyed her. "Are you here to get a good look at the woman you tossed out of your life while the whole bloody village watched?"

He knows he should say something before she begins to hyperventilate. She sounds out of breath. "Willow, please!"

"To hell with you, Graham. I pleased you enough!"

"Willow, I deserve this, and more." He moves a foot closer to her. "I'm worried about you. You don't look well. We can meet tomorrow in my office, or let me come to see you at the house. Please, Willow, this is not the place to settle anything."

Willow senses a need to lean against something cool. She feels faint. Her skin is burning up. There is colourful movement beyond the fence. Her mother's gardens are waving up at her. She can't remember the names of the sturdy flowers that give no hint of fading in this late summer. She leans her face towards the cool hood of the car. Graham's hand grips her wrist. He checks her pulse. Willow turns her head slowly and feels the coolness on the other side of her face. He offers her water to drink, but she doesn't move from the cool smoothness of the metal. For a minute the refreshing sensation dulls the feeling of her emotions. She should be enjoying her meal with her friend Alma. Instead, she picked up the binoculars from the window ledge and focused in on the man at the foot of the mountain. When she saw the New York plates, she knew it was him.

Graham paces in front of his car. His stomach sours with apprehension. His heart is pounding with fear for Willow, who is sprawled on the hood of his car. He wants to hold her in his arms, to comfort her.

Christy's Mountain sends down breaths of cool air mixed with birdsong, a gift for the dysfunctional lovers.

Soon Willow stands up, pumped with fresh anger that mingles with the old. Why has he come to the foot of the mountain? He has a clinic with live-in quarters. Why didn't he go there? She assumes he needed to get as close to her door as possible. She is the one he had to face first on his return. Is he looking for, or expecting, forgiveness? Or perhaps for her to know that he has returned and has not forgotten her, has never forgotten her at all? A man may be capable of deserting a woman at the altar, but love clings savagely to the chambers of a pumping, vital heart. Does he believe that time has softened the years between them?

Willow stands on shaky feet. The words she has planned to say for years are dormant in her mouth. She is tongue-tied by the grief Graham has never witnessed. And then the words spill out, infectious sentences spit into the coming dusk. The sun sinks like a dying inferno between the trees.

"Do you know what the worse kind of coward does?" She sounds as if she is rehearsing a soliloquy.

Graham remains silent, his hands leaning against the roof of his car like a man just arrested for a crime, his eyes fixed on Willow with grave concern. He has no idea how to answer her question.

"The pen-and-paper cowards—they are the worst kind!" She moves closer to him.

Round two is deeper than he expected. Sweat is collecting in the folds of his chins. He breathes in deeply, then exhales fresh air from his lungs as he listens to Willow's short breaths. He is more concerned with her health right now than her anger. He knows she is sick.

"You didn't have the guts to face me, did you, Graham?" He thinks he sees her face soften just a trace. "You left us alone. You knew you'd be well away from the mountain before I got your note."

"I wanted to tell you. I turned back twice the night of the rehearsal as near as I could get to your house. I was hoping to see a light on in your father's work shed. I wanted to speak with him. I knew it was wrong." He stops for air. "I knew it was crazy. Not well thought out. It was the biggest mistake of my life. I am so sorry. I don't know what else I can say or do."

"I'm not interested in what you *almost* did," Willow replies. "It's too late for *almost*."

She is off to the edge of the path in a slow gallop. Graham follows, wishing he'd left the fifty pounds he piled on back in the States. He is about to turn around and go back when she stops suddenly and stands in front of him. They are face to face. She notices the red streaks in his face floating up from under his collar. A blood storm of . . . what? Rage? Exhaustion? High blood pressure?

"You were about to turn back," she says, breathless. "Is someone waiting for you somewhere?"

"Willow, this is getting us nowhere. It's wearing us both out."

"I've been worn out for years," she says.

"I know what you've been through. The death of your parents, then the Millhouses. Death is a heavy weight to carry on your own."

"You're an educated man, Graham Currie, but you have a coward's knowledge. After all these years, you still depend on someone else's sorrow to cover up your own. You've been cruel to the truth. I'll show you a sorrow you haven't faced yet."

"I know my own weakness, Willow. I've wrestled with it for years."

"Good for you. Are you back here to see if I still know mine?"

"I got what I deserved, not what I wanted. Now I want what I've always needed. I didn't come back to the mountain to hurt you again. Is it possible for you to believe that?"

Willow doesn't respond. She turns and resumes her uphill run. A breeze sneaks through the trees and gets her attention. For a time she is unfamiliar with the green surrounding her, the branches brushing deep into her hair, pine cones being swept up by the fiery squirrels. Who says the mountain doesn't have a life of its own? The trees watch everything.

She glances over her shoulder and sees Graham stumbling a few feet behind her. It is much harder now for him to make the incline. His steps are slowing down to a crawl. Poor Graham. More than fifty extra pounds stretches out on his once-slim frame. And his hair, what is left of it, is like dead grass clinging to the edge of a cliff. Willow regains her bearings. They are not far now. She follows the scent of sorrow. She can never forget the treasure that was buried here.

She stops again. She can't hear him behind her anymore. She sees him sitting in the path, mopping his face with a tissue that is too small for his hand.

"Willow." His voice seems to collapse deep inside his chest. "Can we do this some other time?"

"We're almost there."

"I'm not taking another step up this mountain." He has pulled up his legs to rest his heavy head against his knees. His hands dangle between his legs like dead twigs. A canopy of tall elms flaps above his head. He looks like a man on strike.

Graham is well aware of the pain and anger that pulls her forward. He knows that wherever she is headed, she will eventually have to turn around. He will wait. There is still daylight. How much farther can she go by herself?

Suddenly, she is standing over him, her arms on a flight plan all their own. Her fists tighten and open, spreading her long fingers outward. He looks up and begins to say something, but her swift hand covers his mouth.

"It's up the path a bit farther. Get up!" She pulls her hand from his mouth.

"What's so damn urgent that we have to keep going right this minute?" Graham asks, almost pleading. He gets to his feet and stretches out his arms. "Can't we do this some other time?"

"Time is overrated, Graham. Look what it has done to us. I'm a fading spinster, and you . . . We are turning into Mary Ann and John Duncan."

"Willow, please come back down. Go home and get some rest."

"I told you . . . it's not much farther!"

"No, Willow. I'm not going any farther."

He feels her full weight against his back. Her hands tear at his shirt before he can turn around and grab her arms. He has dealt with hysteria many times. It comes in all shapes and sizes. Her hair veils her face. Between the strands, her mouth opens and closes like a goldfish. And then comes her voice, raw, splintered and uncensored. He lets her hands go free. He hears the word. *Miscarriage.*

He shouts at her, "What are you trying to tell me, Willow?"

She may or may not have understood the question. She may have taken offence at the invasion of privacy that was hers for years. She rips into his face with her right fist and watches the blood spider down over his lip—his blood, her baby's blood, trickling like a small finger tracing a map, down the side of the mountain where the cloths of blood were buried and are now, she is certain, a part of the mountain.

It keeps what is fed to it. Willow Alexander has known this since she was five years old. The mountain never released her kite. Her mother must have known it never would.

Willow's voice is hard. Grief doesn't belong in soft sentences. She must get rid of the ghosts. She has to tell him.

"I lost our baby. I buried what was left of its benign existence on the side of the mountain."

She says she should have told him before their wedding day arrived. She was two months pregnant. She watches as he sinks to the ground. His head droops between his knees. His primal cries float with the wind into the trees. His agony, her agony, their agony, is now together on a path of no return.

In the time it takes her to walk back home, Graham's blood has spread between her fingers, first warm, then cold. A red-lined map that leads to where it all began. She moves unsteadily down the mountain. In the distance, she can see Alma walking towards her, her large white arms dangling their loose flesh. She looks worried when she sees the blood on Willow's hand. A cloud follows above Alma's moving figure. A few drops of rain fall. Willow stands still. In her anguish, she sees someone else, someone in white, and she cries out to her mother as Alma sweeps her up in her arms and carries her to the gate.

‡ ‡ ‡

GRAHAM DRIFTS THROUGH his new office and living quarters like an apparition. He wipes the blood from his face with an alcohol swab. There is a deep nail scratch on the edge of his nose. He moves around the room, taps his office equipment, touches the edge of a desk. His face is as blank as a new canvas. The place echoes with silence. He checks his appointment book. There are a few elderly couples, babies and toddlers on the list for the coming week. He must remember to call the hospital in Halifax where he was offered a teaching position, he reminds himself. He had made up his mind to decline the offer before he saw Willow.

How could he not have known Willow's condition when he left Glenmor so suddenly? Her pale face and fatigue at the rehearsal should have alerted him that she was not feeling well. He had worried that she was going to call it off. She had said almost nothing at the rehearsal, and had gone home from the church with her parents and Marjorie. He remembers how she waved to him as they drove away.

He'd parked his car a little distance from the church, escaping like a convict on the lam. Escaped to what? A woman he didn't love. Chronic misery and depression. A great advancement in his career was the only thing he salvaged from the web of deceit he was caught in. And left behind a child he would have loved deeply.

He had turned back that night, but he couldn't go to her door. He wanted to let her know that. He had hoped to see her father in his work shed. Willow was right about one thing: "almost" never makes it to the finish line.

Graham decides to go for a walk down to the shore. A soft south wind blows across his face. His feet sink deep into the sand. Farther down the shore, two young children are engaged in a competition. Who can throw a stone the farthest out to sea? The girl, wearing knee-length shorts, swings her arm in three or four circles before letting the stone fly from her hand. She jumps up and down with delight as her stone makes a soft dip in the calm sea. The boy spits on his stone, twists it around and around in his hands like a pitcher in the big leagues, and aims his throw. It lands two or three feet short of the girl's stone. He kicks the sand. Her laughter is shrill and taunting.

The boy shuffles his feet in the sand as they walk towards Graham. They have gentle faces. The girl, blond and freckled, with quick, intelligent blue eyes. The boy, sandy-haired and fair-skinned, with dark eyes full of curiosity.

"Are you a stranger?" the girl asks. "What happened to your face?" They stand side by side. She nudges the boy slightly to alert him to ask the next question.

"Are you lost, mister?"

Graham smiles at them. He avoids her second question. "I grew up here. I came down here all the time when I was your age."

"Why did you leave?" asks the girl.

"I left to work." Graham coughs to clear his throat.

"I'm never leaving here," the girl says with confidence. "My brother says he's going away after he finishes school." Her brother swats her arm. "We're twins, but nobody believes we're even related when we go to the city. We don't look alike, do we? We're nine, but I'm the oldest."

"Going away is my idea, not yours," says the boy. "I don't want you following me. And Mom said you're not much older than me anyway."

"I don't care where you go. But I know you'll be back. You'll always follow me," she replies, and begins to walk away as their conversation turns to each other.

The girl looks back at Graham. "You still look lost, mister," she says. "Can we help you find somebody you know so you won't be alone?"

CHAPTER TWENTY-EIGHT

===

Wednesday's Children

ALMA MOVES A WASH BASIN TO THE EDGE OF THE table and soaks Willow's bloody hand in cold water. No open cuts are visible on the clean hand. It is not her blood that swirls in the cold water.

"Where did the blood come from, Willow?"

"Graham Currie's face. I punched him when he refused to go up the mountain with me."

"So, it *was* him in that dark car. Why would you want him to go up the mountain with you?"

"There's a lot you don't know."

"Sit down, Willow. I'll pour the tea and you can tell me what you think I should know."

Willow is silent for a minute, then says, "My mother and father never knew. No one knew but me and Kathleen. I believe she suspected it for some time."

"Knew what, dear?"

"That I was pregnant with Graham Currie's child on my wedding day."

Alma's worry lines turn to sadness, a deep, dark sadness that mounts like an approaching storm. Her voice is a damp strip of weary questions. "Graham didn't know that you were carrying his child?"

"No. He didn't know. I planned to tell him on our wedding night."

The teakettle begins to hum in the darkening kitchen. Alma, quick on her feet, turns on the light and then silences the kettle. At the back of the stove, the kettle takes a deep breath and chokes out a last spray of steam. Alma turns to Willow.

"So you told him today? Is that what happened?"

Willow nods. "He just sat there and bawled like a calf, blood running down his chin." Hoarded anger twists the muscles of Willow's face. Her expression alarms Alma. Trapped inside Willow is a rage Alma has not witnessed before.

"Where is he now?" Alma asks.

"On the side of the mountain, where he belongs."

"Why did you want him to go up the mountain?" Alma is cautious now. She fears the answer.

Willow's head swings from side to side. "I wanted him to see where I buried what was left of our child. But he refused to move another inch."

Alma asks no more questions. "I'm going to run a warm bath for you," she says gently. "I can hear some congestion in your chest. You must have a bottle of vapour rub some-where in the house."

"It's just recycled hate you're hearing, Alma. I've waited for years for this moment. Every year that passed, I imagined what my child would have accomplished. How he would have loved and been loved. Graham stole that from me."

"I'm no professional, but I do know that hate is an investment that guarantees no interest. Willow, my dear, you could have had a miscarriage even if you were happily married."

"Are you on his side?"

"The decision Graham made was immature and foolish." Alma's voice softens. "He should have let you know before he made his move. Before you set foot in the church."

"Do you think he would have stayed if I had told him the truth?" Willow whispers.

"Think about it, Willow. He kept the truth from you, and you kept the truth from him. If you want me to be truly honest, I'll tell you what I would tell my own daughters."

Willow slouches further into the kitchen chair. Her damp, clean hand is like a white spider at the end of her bloody sleeve. Alma's voice pierces the kitchen between the gongs being lashed out by the old mantel clock. A robin lands on the windowsill, looks in and flutters off. Alma waltzes a wooden chair around the kitchen and sits directly in front of Willow.

"Look at me, girl."

Willow brushes the hair from her eyes. She stares into Alma's kind but determined face.

"You didn't tell Graham you were pregnant because you were afraid."

Willow attempts to protest but is hushed up.

"He didn't tell you he was fooling around with someone who could greatly benefit his career because he was afraid. Guess what? Two frightened people met for a wedding rehearsal. And the rest is history. But as I'm sure you know, Willow Alexander, there's no rehearsal for life. Do you even know what you were afraid of?"

Willow takes a deep breath. "I was afraid he'd marry me for the baby's sake. If I kept quiet, then I would know it was me he wanted."

"Good planning, my dear. If he'd married you for the child's sake, what did you think would have happened?"

Willow doesn't respond.

"You must have suspected there was something in the air."

Willow considers and nods. "I suspected something had changed. He wasn't coming home as often as he used to. He made excuses for me not to go up on weekends to visit. He was on edge. He wasn't the same Graham who left Glenmor."

"Well, I for one am never surprised by the raw misery of romance. Time changes a person. Most brides only think of matching shoes and what the first marriage kiss will be like. I believe you knew all along what to expect: a no-show. You have been angry at yourself all these years. Graham is simply the sketch you kept around until you were ready to fill in the details. And yet the real reason may shock you one of these days. I'm making assumptions here, child. I don't know what was going on in his mind."

"Why didn't he ask me, if he suspected I was pregnant?"

"I can think of a few reasons. One is obvious. Given the amount of blood you drained out of him today, he probably feared for his life!"

Willow watches the heavy weight of Alma's shoulders slacken. Her hands rise to cover her red face. A burst of laughter comes from behind her spread fingers like light notes from white piano keys. Then Willow feels the pull of Alma's strong arms. Her body moves to nestle against the frame of a woman who at the moment is the mediator between love and loss. Willow can hear her mother's voice and Kathleen's voice mingle in a far-off distance. Alma's voice whispers along Willow's skin and into her ear.

"Wednesday's child is full of woe."

Willow doesn't remember telling Alma that she and Graham were both born on a Wednesday.

CHAPTER TWENTY-NINE

==

United by Illness

G RAHAM EXAMINES THE BRUISE DEEPENING UNDER a tender swell on the edge of his nose. It will be gone, he's sure, before he opens the office for patients the following week. The broken vessel on the inside of his nose will be healed by then too.

There is still enough sunlight left in the day to spread a yellow hue over the acres of land that surround his newly acquired clinic and living quarters. He stands on Kathleen Millhouse's balcony and looks around.

He sees the lone figure of a woman walking away from the soundless sea, long hair, dark and turbulent, swaying down her back. A small basket in one hand rocks lazily against her slight frame. He wonders what's in the basket. Seashells or sea glass? Sand dollars, perhaps? Frivolous thoughts run rampant in Graham's head. He is a man who has shed enough blood for one day. He has collected enough secrets and sorrow, and is ready to start a new chapter in his life. The possibility that this new life might include Willow, the love of his life, is not looking good, though.

Graham pours himself a strong drink, single-malt Scotch whisky that he purchased when he crossed the border. He forgot he had stuffed it into his duffle bag. The drink rolls down his throat like peated honey. Soon a ballad whistled behind his teeth sings its way into the empty room. It is a happy song, one he and Willow and Marjorie sang once when they were around a bonfire at the beach.

A ringing phone ends his ballad. It is his mother, asking why he didn't call as soon as he arrived. She has made a special dinner for him.

"Do you have food in that place?" she asks. "And by the way, Polina phoned to ask about you. She said she's coming down for a visit."

"I wouldn't advise that she travel here alone," Graham answers, "and don't bring her to my place if she does come."

"That's not very polite of you, Graham. The girl is just concerned. And why shouldn't she travel alone? That doesn't make sense. She's educated and a professional."

"The girl is no concern of mine anymore. End of conversation. I'm going to bed." He hangs up the phone abruptly.

His mother's checking up on him annoys him. Polina's checking up annoys him. This is one thing Willow couldn't be accused of. She never checked up on him, never con-

tacted him. She avoided him at all costs when he used to
return home for visits. She always remained elusive. She
was no doubt suffering from depression. Yet she can still
fight with a fist as mean as a mule kick, her green eyes on
her target like a sniper. Graham's mind is a trap of anger and
remorse and regret. Willow is the crown jewel of his desire.
She was his elusive mountain lover who always chose her
own heights. He never took advantage of her. She knew the
laws of love. And he could not tame her, no more than he
could have tamed the mountain.

He thinks back to the wedding rehearsal. She must
have noticed his worn, wrinkled shirt and jeans that day.
Her father certainly had. He watched Murdoch Alexander's
eyes roam from the collar of his plaid shirt to the cuffs of
his jeans. He knew something. He expected Willow to ask
with a smirk if he had robbed a scarecrow on the way to
the church. But she said very little, observed very little. She
simply fit her hand into his when he told her he loved her
as they stood at the foot of the altar for their rehearsal. This
memory shatters him the most. Willow always spoke best
with her hands. Like the way she waved at him when she
rode home with her father and mother after the rehearsal.
Almost a bride, almost a wife. What had he said to her?
Not "Until tomorrow, Willow." Not "Have a good sleep."
He said nothing. He had not spoken a word to her when
she left. He spent the night in a small motel on his way
back to Halifax. He drank himself into a stupor and woke

at eleven the next morning from a nightmare to the sounds of a brawling couple in the next room. He took his nightmare dream with him into the cold shower, but it refused to drown.

The phone rings again, annoying him further. He considers not answering it, but instinct forces his hand to stop the damn ringing. There is an unfamiliar woman's voice on the other end.

"Graham, this is Alma MacInnis. I'm staying at Willow's house. I'm very concerned about her breathing. It doesn't sound right."

"I'll be right there."

‡ ‡ ‡

WHEN GRAHAM ARRIVES at the house, Alma opens the door to a heavy-set man with his own breathing problems. Beads of sweat race down his forehead. His voice is hurried. "Where is she?"

Graham finds Willow propped up against three pillows, shallow breaths rising and falling as if she were a young child trying to blow up a balloon. The room is as hot as a steam bath. Graham throws the heavy quilt she is wrapped in against the wall.

"Bring me a basin of cold water and some cloths!" He does not look up at Alma when he asks for the water. "And open that window, for God's sake!"

He knows what he is dealing with even before he checks her lungs. Left lung infected, right lung congested, a feverish blush. Her hair is tied back. Her wild green eyes blinking at the man in front of her. For all she knows, Graham is in her home to finish the battle.

"I suspect you have pneumonia in one lung, Willow," Graham says professionally. "I'll get antibiotics into you soon enough." Graham's voice is apologetic, as though he were the cause of her illness too.

"Go to hell, Graham. Who invited you here, anyway?" Willow mutters.

"Your very wise friend. You should be grateful to her. This is nothing to fool around with."

"Neither are you, Graham."

"Save your strength, or I'll call an ambulance and have you carted off to a hospital. It's probably where you should be!"

Willow doesn't reply.

Before Graham leaves, he speaks to Alma. "I'll call the druggist and pick up the medicine."

Alma stares into Graham's round, aging face. The cut on the side of his nose is visible. She notes that his bedside manner is professional. After he leaves, Alma listens to Willow's broken breaths at the open door, then checks the damp white cloth covering her eyes.

Alma leaves and clears the table in the kitchen. Graham will be returning soon. She makes a fresh pot of tea. She noticed that Graham looked tired. "A hot meal is what he needs right now," she thinks, and she is more than willing to feed the man.

"I want to keep an eye on her condition," he tells Alma when he gets back to the house. "Would staying the night be out of the question?"

Alma knows Willow would not allow it, but she also knows having him here will take a great worry off her shoulders, and so she agrees. She invites Graham to sit down for a meal. He barely speaks as he sips his tea and eats his chowder, except to say, "It's good that you're here, Alma. I doubt Willow would have phoned me. I hope Marjorie is doing well, and the rest of your family as well."

Alma nods her thanks. "She didn't call me either, Graham," she replies. "It was me who phoned her. I suspected something was wrong. I know her well. She's a very proud woman."

"Proud women can die from pneumonia just like everyone else," he replies sombrely.

Alma observes Graham's face. It is a kind but troubled face. Flushed. Perhaps because of the bowl of steaming fish chowder, or the revelations of the day, or what is left of his life and Willow's. Perhaps all of the above. The truth can wound a person as much as a lie. And Alma knows he is consumed by the new truth about the loss of the child. And Willow is wounded by his return. There is a weight between his leaving and returning that she could not balance. What Willow has to offer him now is a part of her physical self, her wounded lungs. Graham is the one in control at the moment. Her body is his to heal. The lovers are reunited by illness, which will keep him under her roof for the night.

Alma treads carefully around their conversations. She doesn't dislike Graham Currie. He is polite and well-mannered. And she stays out of his way when he tends to Willow. But she does not miss the look in his eyes when he drops his hand over her forehead or when he holds her wrist to take her pulse. Alma sets up the foldaway cot for him in the hallway, just outside Willow's room. He returns for supper at the end of each day, and in the end, he stays over for four nights.

He thanks Alma for her help, but Alma knows it isn't her help that he is grateful for, but her trust in him as a healer. On his final morning at the house, he asks Alma to take Willow to the hospital for a chest X-ray.

Willow mutters a barely audible "Thank you" to Graham before he leaves. She does not look up to face him.

===

CHAPTER THIRTY

The Appointment

A WEEK LATER, AFTER ALMA HAS LEFT, MRS. Welsh returns. Willow is fond of Mrs. Welsh and owes a debt of gratitude to her for the care she gave Rhona in her illness. And Mrs. Welsh needs the extra money, Willow knows. She doesn't want to tell her she feels stronger now and can manage on her own, that an extra hand is no longer necessary every day.

The first thing Mrs. Welsh does when she arrives is tear into the rooms, disinfecting walls and windows and closets. She takes beds apart and scrubs them with bleach, and it makes her happy to see Willow's health improving as she cleans. She worries that Willow could have a relapse and believes the illness might be waiting for the chance to return with a new vengeance. She advises Willow to take slow walks near the mountain to fill her lungs with fresh country air.

"I see that Currie fella made his way back," she says

one day in the kitchen, oblivious to the raw wounds she is inflaming. Willow doesn't tell her that Graham tended to her for four days. "Some nerve, I'd say, after the trick he pulled on you! But still, people say he's a good doctor. Nice and kind when you go there, especially to kids. He just loves the kids. I can't say what he's like with women. Didn't go myself. He could fire a bottle of pills at you and throw you out for bothering him, for all I know."

Willow tugs her heavy sweater down from the hook and slips it on. She asks Mrs. Welsh to leave the door open when she leaves for home. Then Willow escapes into the light breeze that is tumbling down from the mountain.

Willow has her red boots on. Her feet feel light, even with the heavy socks, as she strolls along the road. The iron gates of the Journey's End Cemetery loom in the distance. The morning started with a soggy drip of intermittent rain, but now the sun, fresh-faced and bold, traces the damp headstones like a warm hand.

Willow hasn't been here for a couple of months. A new growth of green grass now shades her parents' graves.

"Do the dead know you're here?" Willow wonders. "Is that why people return over and over to visit the graves of their loved ones?" She's not sure. But she finds the silence here inviting. She stands back from her parents' graves, smiling slightly. She imagines her mother's voice:

Your hair, Willow, your strawberry-blond mane, could use a good shine.

Willow doesn't imagine her father's voice. It's his smile she remembers. His smile spoke before he ever said a word. A stretched-out smile with no teeth showing meant no. Flashing white teeth framed by full, thick lips meant yes. Life's decisions were that simple for Murdoch Alexander.

Willow suddenly hears music and turns to see where it's coming from. A truck makes its way slowly towards her. The driver's arm, tanned and muscled, is slung out the window. He taps his hand against the dented door in rhythm with the velvet voice of a singer she doesn't recognize. A hand-painted sign is scrawled on the side of the truck: CONSTRUCTION & DESTRUCTION, INC. The truck stops beside the Alexander graves. A grin is locked on the driver's handsome face. He's barely out of his teens.

"Hope I'm not disturbing you, miss," he says politely. "I got orders to square off a plot big enough to sink three stiffs."

Willow is taken by surprise. "You mean here? So close?"

"That's what the purchase order says. You only get what you pay for. The rest is up for grabs. Some woman ordered it a while back."

"I hope you don't have them in the back of your truck!"

He chuckles. "You're pretty funny for an older lady!"

"I wasn't trying to be funny," Willow replies, annoyed. "I'd just like to know who will be buried so close to me."

The kid shrugs. "Search me, lady. I just plot 'em. I don't plant 'em."

Willow can still hear the music as she walks by Mary Ann's and John Duncan's graves. Mary Ann's headstone is leaning at a slight angle, tilted towards John Duncan's stone. It looks as if she has a secret to tell him. Willow turns and walks farther down the path towards her grand-parents' graves, and tries to push aside the encounter with the young man, who is squaring off the new plots so close to her parents' resting place.

‡ ‡ ‡

THREE WEEKS LATER, Willow walks into a hair salon and asks to see a shade of strawberry-blond colouring. The stylist lifts a few strands of Willow's fading hair as though she were pulling weeds.

"We just got a new shade in," she says, as a soft bubble from her chewing gum rests on her lower lip. "It's called Strawberry Explosion."

After her appointment, Willow drives home along the mountain in the warm September sun. She glances repeat-edly into the rear-view mirror, surprised at how she looks. She's never paid much attention to her physical appearance before, but now she's noticing the way the mirror is flush-ing out her father's full smile from her lips. And looking back at her are her mother's large round eyes. To Willow's amusement, the bone structure of her chin reminds her of the Croppers. She's never noticed it before. She has never been one to fuss over her looks. But dear Kathleen warned her not to let her beauty suffer.

"This world needs beauty and colour, Willow. Take care of yourself. Don't waste your time on regret!"

Willow's mother was always powdered and fluffed. She took pride in looking good for her man. Perhaps that's why her father always smiled.

Willow's new hair is a shade darker than the hair of the young girl flying a kite at dawn thirty-five years ago. The hairdresser has cut her hair and given it a sassy bob style. Soft bangs fall like feathers over her forehead. Her thick, unruly eyebrows are now shaped into perfect arches. Mascara darkens her lashes and blush tints her cheeks. Her lips are now a pinkish-orange shade that complements her hair. What possessed her to have these things done? Why now? She does not allow herself the possibility that her sudden interest in her appearance has anything to do with Graham Currie. Does she want to let him know what the girl he left behind really looks like?

When Willow arrives home, there is a note taped to her door.

Willow, I would like to see you at my office regarding your test results. Please call as soon as possible. Graham.

‡ ‡ ‡

GRAHAM ANSWERS THE office door wearing rumpled track pants and an oversized Yale sweatshirt. He's shed some weight since returning home, she notices. Willow steps into the newly decorated office and notices her old desk is gone. It has been replaced by a sleek, curved counter. There is now shelving everywhere for the patient files. The walls are painted a bright blue. Willow thinks it looks like a bus station. The smell of coffee drifts out from the bright-yellow kitchen.

There are dark circles pooled under Graham's eyes. Willow thinks he looks tired. But she notices he's been in the sun. His face and the top of his head are a deeper shade than the last time she saw him. The colour suits him. "If he would buy some new clothes," she thinks, "he might look almost presentable."

"You've made a lot of changes," she says.

"So have you," he replies, then instantly regrets it. Graham takes a seat behind his new teak desk and motions for Willow to sit as well. He shuffles some papers on his desk before continuing. "Uh, I wanted to go over your X-ray reports with you."

"So you said in your note."

He clears his throat. "Yes, well, there appears to be some fluid on your right lung. Have you been having any trouble breathing?"

"No. Only when I run marathons up the mountain," Willow answers with a straight face.

Graham smiles briefly. "Well, it's probably nothing to worry about, but I'm going to suggest you come back"—he clears his throat—"for another checkup in two weeks. Just to make sure."

"Make sure of what?"

"To make sure . . . it's not something serious. That's all." Graham is a terrible liar. "You can refuse if you wish. It's your choice. Your lungs."

"Are you saying I can choose whether I want congestion or not?"

He sighs. "You know what I mean, Willow."

He lowers his eyes again, scribbles a date on an appointment card and hands it to her. He feels she's mocking him behind her beautiful eyes. But at the same time, he still senses that the hatred he saw in her eyes when he first arrived back home seems to have softened a little. Or has she just replaced it with the mockery? It's hard to tell.

"I hope you haven't started smoking, Willow."

"No. I just check ashtrays," she says, eyeing the clean ashtray on his desk. "Have you *stopped* smoking, Graham?"

"Yes. Years ago. The ashtray is a leftover vice. A reminder." His face is serious now. "I know it's personal, and I don't want to have you relive a sad event." She knows what's coming, and he takes a deep breath before asking, "Did you see a doctor after your miscarriage?"

She looks at him, eye to eye. "Of course I did. In Halifax. Everything is fine. No complications. He said I was healthy

enough to have more children. But I was twenty-four then."
She slips the appointment card into her purse and stands up.

Graham stands up too, then asks, tentatively, expecting
rejection, "Would you like a cup of coffee, or do you check
coffee pots too?"

Willow laughs. It's the first time he has seen her laugh
since they were young.

"I guess it wouldn't hurt. One cream."

Graham hurries to the kitchen, half-afraid she'll be gone
when he gets back with the coffee. He stands in the kitchen
doorway and looks over at her. He knows he can't tell her
how beautiful she looks without making a fool of himself. He can't say how pleased he is that she's beginning to
make some changes in her life, that she is healthy. He can't
tell her that her lungs are as clear and sharp as her tongue.
He's already crossed the line of propriety by lying to her.
Keeping her wounded is his only way of keeping her near.

Graham passes Willow a gold mug with a hound dog
painted on it. The handle is shaped like a bone. Willow sits
with her back to the wall in a new padded chair and sips
the hot, excellent coffee. Before they can begin speaking
again, the telephone rings. Graham stumbles to reach it
and the coffee in his hand splashes brown spots all over his
paperwork.

It's a short conversation. Then he says, "I'm sorry,
Willow. I have to go on an emergency call. Please stay
and finish your coffee." He grabs his bag off the floor and

clamps it shut. "Would you make sure the door is closed when you leave?" At the door, he glances back over his shoulder, hoping against hope that she will still be there, in the new red chair, when he gets back.

After he leaves, Willow holds the dog mug firmly as she walks up the stairs. On the landing, she pauses before moving along the hallway. She walks down the long hall and opens the door to the balcony. She checks the parking lot. It's empty. Graham is gone. The door to the Millhouses' former bedroom is open. The walls are now painted an off-white. An array of green plants in various wooden and metal holders form a small jungle across the double doors to the balcony. Beside Graham's bed, an old wicker table holds a collection of seashells, a piece of driftwood and a mother-of-pearl picture frame.

Willow creeps closer. In the picture frame is a photo of Willow. The one and only photo ever taken of her on her wedding day. She picks it up. Her heart is pounding. In the photo, part of her veil is wrapped around her neck like a scarf. A circle of pearls is sculpted into a small crown resting on her head. One of her hands holds the railing. In the other hand are wildflowers, tied together with a piece of lace, pressed firmly against her stomach. Her hair is pulled back into a soft bun. She had forgotten—or perhaps she never knew—how happy and beautiful she was on that day and how much promise shone in her eyes. Her eyes held the clarity and love of a woman protecting something precious.

She had not yet felt the first kick of her baby, yet she had already chosen his name, sure it would be a boy.

Willow removes the photo from the frame. On the back, in black ink, is a brief message.

Graham: You told me at the wedding rehearsal you wanted to see her on her wedding day because you wouldn't be there.

I took this picture for you as Willow was going into the church. I kept your secret. Isn't that what family is for?

Cousin Mari

Willow takes a deep breath. Why would a man, leaving his bride at the altar, want a photo of her in her wedding gown? She wants to tear up the photo and burn it with all the others. Yet another part of her longs to keep it safe. She deserves this one memento of herself and her unborn baby. This moment of mother and child. Graham has no right to it. She places the photo back in the frame, so Graham won't know she's been in his room. Willow will have to think of some other way to get it.

Willow closes the door behind her when she leaves the clinic and walks down to the shore. She shuffles along the sand in her bare feet to cool off. She reaches down and picks up a stick of driftwood and carves the name Gabriel into the wet sand.

‡ ‡ ‡

GRAHAM IS DESPONDENT when he returns to find Willow gone. It had been more than a month since he last saw her, and now he is afraid it might be another month before he sees her again. He's already deceived her into a visit. What did she think when she found his note on her door? He hadn't really expected her to show up. But he saw how she looked at him. She knew she didn't have to worry about congestion. She asked no questions about her health, and she hadn't exhibited any panic. He was relieved when she didn't ask to see the report.

Graham pulls his sad body up the stairs, an ache in his legs slowing him down. "You need more exercise, man, more exercise." He frowns at his own advice. A hot shower soothes his aching bones. It also scalds his sunburnt head, and he swears out loud in pain. He looks in the full-length mirror, discouraged. What does his body have to offer a woman? He makes his way to the bed and pulls back the covers. He has reached a crossroads in his life and he's afraid. He is working on his physical problems. But he knows he should see someone soon about his other problems, his despair and longing. "What keeps a man in a dead marriage for ten years?" he wonders, before answering his own question out loud: "A dead man, you fool, a dead man."

He reaches for Willow's picture and holds it tightly.

It is still in his hand when he awakes the next morning.

‡ ‡ ‡

Willow lies in the shadows of her bedroom and pulls the sheet up under her chin. The image of her wedding photo floats in her mind, keeping her awake. Her heart aches deeply for her parents, for her friend Kathleen. She could have gone to her. Kathleen had opened many doors for her after Graham left, and when she lost her parents. She shook her finger at Willow when she asked if she could keep one punch in reserve for the man. "One punch can lead to two, Willow," she had warned.

If she had ignored Graham's note, she wouldn't have gone to his office. She wouldn't have crept up the stairs like a voyeur when he left. She knew he was playing games with her about the X-ray report, and she played along with him. Why had she gone to his office? Did she want him to see how good she could look when she dressed up? Was she just teasing his sorrow to the brink of madness? What would she do with his madness when it came? She curses her weakness. Why should she even care what Graham Currie does?

She longs for her father's strength. Nobody broke Murdoch Alexander. How could she have believed she was so strong this whole time? It haunts her still to remember what she did with her wedding dress. It was a work of art made especially for her by her mother, and yet she destroyed it out of anger. She marinated it in kerosene before striking the match. The satin and lace of the eloquent bodice caught the first flame. The fire sounded like crying as it spread to the full skirt.

Willow remembers a night shortly before her mother died when the sky was so white with stars they seemed to hold the world still. A half moon had smiled down over the mountain as she watched her mother sleeping, her soft breaths rising and falling under a white sheet as though she were whispering to the stars. Willow knelt beside her bed and wrapped her in her arms.

"Thank you, Mother, for your works of art, my kite, my cake, my gown, my life with you and my father. I should never have destroyed anything that you put a hand to."

Willow was walking out of the room when she heard her mother's feeble voice. "You're welcome, child."

In the morning, Willow calls Alma, hoping to talk out the tangles in her head. Alma listens patiently to her latest adventures. The hairdo and makeup. The visit to Graham's office. The hound-dog coffee mugs. And the heart of her turmoil, the photo.

"I have to have that photo, Alma."

"Why don't you ask him for it?"

"Then he'd know I was snooping." Willow sighs.

"After all that's happened, dear, I don't think that will make much difference."

"He looks terrible."

"Willow, you may not agree with what I have to say, but I will say it anyway," Alma says, ending the small talk. "A liar will never connect with his real emotions. When you try to dissolve one lie with another, no progress is ever made. Both of you have to start telling the truth. Now. With or without help."

"I wish Graham Currie had stayed away from Glenmor," Willow adds wistfully.

"No, you don't! You couldn't wait to nail him. You weren't satisfied until you spilled his blood on the mountain. And what did you get out of it? Revenge is a dirty, calculated emotion when it spills over. It splashed the two of you." Alma pauses for a breath, then keeps going. "And what do you believe that photo will do for you? Bring back your youth? Your wedding day? No, Willow. It will only bring back heartache, and God knows there's enough of that in both of your lives already. Graham's cousin had no business sending that photo to Graham. She must be an idiot. Imagine what it did to him all these years. No wonder the man is on the verge of despair."

"I honestly thought the photo would give me some kind of strength," Willow says. "I don't know what to do."

Alma hesitates, then replies: "Go to him. Tell him the truth, and maybe he'll fall into the habit of truth telling himself. He's not an evil man. He is a good man. He'll probably be relieved. And think of it this way: You lost both parents and survived. You lost your child, and then your dear friend Kathleen died along with her husband, and here you still are, breathing, walking, talking and making plans for a new beginning. You must remember all the people who loved and relied on you for comfort and keep going. Willow, I can understand your fears. But I say what must be said to strengthen you. You are stronger than your imagination leads you to believe."

CHAPTER THIRTY-ONE

==

A Tilted Tombstone

WILLOW SITS ON THE NEW RED CHAIR FACING Graham. She called and asked for an after-hours appointment. Of course, he agreed. He wanted to see her again. He is wearing the same track suit he wore the last time she visited. Willow is wearing no makeup, but her hair is still Strawberry Explosion. Steam is rising from the two hound-dog mugs of coffee on Graham's desk. Willow tells him she wants to see the X-ray report. Graham panics when she asks. He ruffles through the papers on his desk, then gets up and takes her file from the shelf before sitting back down.

"Never mind, Graham. I know the results," Willow admits.

Graham closes the file. "In other words, you know I was lying." He fumbles nervously for his coffee and it splashes on Willow's file.

Willow stands. "I'll get a cloth."

"I'm sorry, Willow," Graham says, looking directly at her. "I honestly don't know what to say to you anymore. I told you the truth on the mountain and you nailed me. I fudged the truth on your report and you figured it out. I'm to blame for it all. I've been lying to you and to myself far too long. It never stops, and I . . . ." He hesitates, then starts again. "I even left a bouquet of flowers on Mary Ann's grave with a note for you to meet me there, like a lovesick teenager." He takes a deep breath. "Jesus, I was a doctor by then. And now my mother tells me that Polina wants to drop by. For a visit."

This statement piques Willow's interest. "Your mother?" she asks. "You don't have to take orders from your mother ever again. You are not in grade school. Remember what she was like in those days, Graham?"

"I told her not to bring her near me. Sometimes I wonder why I put up with any of this stress."

Willow leans forward and clears her throat, ready to make a statement of her own. "I should have told you I was carrying your child. You had a right to know. But the truth never comes up when we need it the most. I felt things had started to change. You didn't come home as often. You made excuses, saying you had too much work to do. I knew something was stopping you, but I didn't think it was another woman. Graham, you had a right to know about your child. But I was afraid it would have been your only reason for staying with me. I should have trusted you."

He stares at her in disbelief. Had she really just said she was sorry, or did he just imagine it? "Oh, my dearest Willow, if only you had intervened. If only."

Willow continues talking. "Why did you come back? Your mother drives you crazy. What's here for you?"

Graham ignores her questions. Slowly, he gets up from behind his desk and walks to the window. His back is to Willow. She watches the tremble in his hands as he begins to speak.

"I was greedy enough to take up her offer of research to advance my career. I didn't love her." His voice rises in anger. "Then she trapped me in a lie, used me and threatened me. I was about to lose everything I had worked for. I felt guilty because I had been so stupid. She used me and I lost you. That's all I can say about it."

The silence that follows stretches into minutes. Willow's voice is impatient and dark when she asks, "Did you happen to notice the colour of the wool she pulled over your eyes?" She is sorry for being so blunt the minute she speaks.

"You wouldn't believe me if I told you the truth about the last ten years." There is a tear and an unsettling plea in Graham's voice when he speaks.

"That's possible, Graham. I don't trust my own feelings anymore either." Willow stares down at the lonely hound dog on the mug.

Graham turns from the window and stares at her like a child about to be left at school on the first day of kindergarten. Willow doesn't ask any more questions about his ex-wife's visit. Willow has had an uneasy feeling about Polina's intentions in light of his objections. She changes the subject for Graham's sake as well as her own.

"I saw the flowers on Mary Ann's grave," Willow says. "But the wind must have carried away your note."

"Would you have met me there?"

"I don't know." Willow gets up to leave. She is unsure how to answer him.

"I have something you might like to have," Graham says when she doesn't answer. "It's a photo of you in your—"

"I know, Graham. I went upstairs the last time I was here. I can't lie to you anymore. It wears me out."

Graham is surprised by what she says. It is unlike Willow to trespass into someone else's private space.

"I want you to have it, Graham. If it brings you some kind of comfort, please keep it."

"It does. I appreciate it, Willow."

Willow prepares to leave. Graham takes the hound-dog mugs to the kitchen and catches a glimpse of his face in the mirror over the sink. A warm light flickers in his eyes. A slow shiver wrinkles his spine. The look in Willow's eyes when she told him to keep the photo, the quiet resolution of truth, makes him realize she is stronger than he ever could be.

"I have to get going. I'm taking Mrs. Welsh shopping in the morning. We are going to Sydney." Her offering is unrehearsed, a spur-of-the-moment question: "Is there anything you need?"

"Can I answer that question honestly?" he asks shyly.

"Sometime soon, Graham, I will ask you again. I'm not ready for your answer now."

Her voice is calm. He is devastated by her lack of an answer. He's never felt this way about any other woman. Her silence, her anger at his return when he saw her at the mountain. How the hell could he have left Willow for so long?

After Willow leaves, Graham lies on his bed, thinking of the recurring dream he has had since returning to Glenmor. In the dream, he watches Willow walk up the middle aisle of an empty church in her gown. There are wildflowers all over the floor. She scatters them with her feet as she walks. Then she reaches down and picks up a single flower and places it on a closed coffin at the foot of the altar.

‡ ‡ ‡

WILLOW WALKS THE long route home, passes the cemetery, then changes her mind and turns back. She enters the cemetery and strolls along the clean paths beside the tombstones, thinking of the love stories of the people she's known. Her mother walked this path as a child with her twin dolls in a pram, safe in the knowledge that ghosts never appear in the light. She recalls how her mother carried her magic wand as an additional safeguard. Willow smiles at the thought of her father falling under the spell of Rhona's magic wand when they wed.

She also remembers Alma telling her that she and her husband had their wedding pictures taken in the grave-yard. "We made sure there were no funerals that day." She laughed. "The trees were in full bloom. Dressed for the occasion." Alma was always a pragmatist, and everything worked out for her.

Willow recalls once seeing a photo of James and Kathleen Millhouse's wedding. Camera-shy James, uncomfortable in the spotlight, looked only at his bride. Two gifted minds who remained together until their time ran out.

Willow remembers the lovely Bella, her grandmother, the bride in satin, naive in life but loved to death under the quilt that stitched their lives together in marriage.

And she thinks of Mrs. Welsh, spellbound by her husband's words, and who was introduced, over tea, to the magic of books, as they fell in love between the pages.

At the base of Mary Ann's tilting headstone, Willow finds a place to sit and leans lightly against it. She remembers the day she found the bouquet on Mary Ann's grave. She reminds herself to call the young man from the construction company to ask him to straighten up the stone. It is the least she can do for the ghost woman who has intrigued her and Graham for so many years. Willow turns her attention to John Duncan, who is next to her, his heart rumoured to have died once hopelessness emptied his spirit of belief. Willow will not have Mary Ann fall for him now. It's too late for that.

CHAPTER THIRTY-TWO

One Crow Sorrow

WILLOW IS MAKING UP AN EXTRA BATCH OF FOOD for Sorrow and his friends when a dark shadow passes by her window. She hopes the crows have not arrived too early. A stranger appears on her doorstep. It's raining and Willow opens the door. She eyes the frail, freckle-faced woman who stands before her. She seems lost. Her voice has a thin edge.

"Are you Willow Alexander?" the woman asks.

"Yes, I am," Willow replies.

"I am Dr. Polina Rebane. I'm a Harvard graduate. I was told that I would find my husband, Dr. Graham Currie, here. I would like him returned to me."

For a moment Willow is speechless. She shuffles her feet, perplexed by this encounter. "So here she is," Willow thinks. Polina. She is not what Willow expected. This woman on her doorstep looks worn, drained and remote.

"Well, Dr. Polina Rebane, Harvard graduate," Willow says, smiling, "I'm afraid I don't collect husbands. Crows maybe. But not husbands. You've landed on the wrong doorstep."

Polina's eyelids flutter. "I went to the clinic and they said he left for the evening."

"That may be true, but I have no knowledge of his whereabouts. Please come in and sit down. Or look around if you wish. The rain in Glenmor has no sympathy, even for Harvard graduates."

Polina steps inside and removes her raincoat and boots at Willow's request.

"Come into the kitchen. You'll be more comfortable there. I'll make a pot of tea," Willow says.

"I drink only organic tea," Polina replies flatly. "That other junk corrodes the stomach. I always carry my own." She takes a teabag from her handbag and passes it to Willow.

Willow smiles and drops two of her own teabags into the pot, pocketing Polina's. She glances at her uninvited guest, who is watching the rain beating against the window. Her dark hair is tucked under the collar of her wrinkled blouse. She looks like a crumbling doll that was left out in the rain.

When the tea is ready, they sit down facing each other at the kitchen table. Willow detects a smouldering flame in Polina's eyes, just waiting for a spark. "This woman has set more than one fire in her mind," she thinks.

Willow speaks softly to her, and cautiously watches her every move.

"Tea tastes good in your little house," Polina remarks. "It must be the water."

"Are you hungry, Polina?"

"No. And I probably couldn't eat what you cooked anyway. I'm not used to mountain food."

Willow grins. "How did you know where my little house was? I see you don't have a car."

"My mother-in-law dropped me off at your gate. She said she'll pick me up later. She said Graham may be here. You've been to his office a few times. He made coffee for you before you left. Mrs. Currie is aware of your every move."

"You said you came to my little house to look for your husband. I was under the impression that Graham was your *ex*-husband."

Polina's face explodes. Her little eyes dart back and forth from the window to Willow's face in disbelief. "You have been misinformed, you whore!" she shouts. "My Graham would never leave me for someone who looks like you. You think you're beautiful with your dyed red hair and eyebrows like a plucked chicken. You're uneducated and skinny and homely and poor. You don't even have organic teabags. You believe you just have to smile at a man and his intestines coil like a snake."

Willow plans her next move. She knows she must be careful. She has trampled on a live wire. "That's true,

Polina, I don't have organic teabags. But I believe you."

"My Graham and I own our own clinic. We are very successful. My mother-in-law was right about you—you were always in love with Graham. And you lured him back here for an encore."

"We went to school together, Polina. Graham and I," Willow replies, trying to stay calm.

"School wouldn't stop you from falling in love, you idiot. It was probably your breeding ground."

"That could be true, Polina. You're very smart," Willow says. "Did you have a special friend at school?"

Polina's face twists. "No, they made fun of me. The kids in boarding school laughed at my thick glasses and my superior mind."

"That wasn't very kind of them."

"I'm sure if you had been there, you would have made fun of me too."

"No, I don't think I would have, Polina. I probably would have liked you and been your friend. I'm not fond of people who hurt others for no reason."

"What's with all the questions, you idiot? You're trying to get a reading on me and you don't even know what chapter you're on. I'm too smart for you and you know it."

Willow stands up and keeps the table between them. She knows she's dealing with someone who has to be treated delicately, and she gets into position to protect herself.

"I do not have your husband here, Polina," Willow says

quietly. "He's probably on a house call or at the hospital in the city. You can see him when he returns. I will bring you back to Mrs. Currie's house if you wish."

Polina stares at her blindly, clearly wondering whether to believe her or not. "He is my husband, not yours. He didn't marry you. I made sure of that."

"What did you do, Polina? How did you make sure he didn't marry me?" Willow asks in a quiet voice, to keep the conversation going.

"I made him love me. He raped me the first time he came to my apartment. I told him I would report him to his superiors if he didn't marry me and move to New York. I saved his medical career."

"Did he really rape you, Polina? If he did, it wasn't very nice of him to hurt you like that."

"No," Polina says, her face a mass of confusion. "No, my Graham wouldn't do anything like that. He loves me! How dare you spread lies about my husband by putting mean words in my mouth."

"I wouldn't lie to you, Polina. It's not worth it to lie to people."

Willow grips the edge of her chair. So this was what made Graham leave so suddenly. He would have lost it all because of this poor, delusional soul.

"So you tricked him, Polina. You made him believe that he could lose his right to practise medicine." Willow feels a fire ignite in her own mind now that she knows the truth.

She takes a deep breath to cool down. She can't blame this ill woman. But the idea of Mrs. Currie bringing this woman to her house infuriates her. Mrs. Currie could not have missed the signs of her mental illness, which Polina displays like a billboard.

Polina suddenly jumps from her chair and runs into the pantry before Willow can reach her. Polina stands in the pantry doorway, a knife in her hand. Its shiny blade moves like a pendulum in Polina's slight hand. Her hair is down over her face. The despair in her voice is clear as she spits it out through the strands of hair.

"Women like you make me sick! How dare you try and steal my husband from me. Why don't you get a husband for yourself? Or is someone else's flesh more appealing to you?"

Willow hears a car pull up in her driveway. She looks out the window and sees that it is Mrs. Currie.

"Good timing, you old bag," Willow hisses under her breath.

Polina awkwardly advances from the pantry. Her direction is confused. She stumbles as Willow tries to grab the knife from her hand. Polina pulls her hand back. The blade grazes Willow's hand. She grabs Polina's long, wet hair and Polina drops the knife. Willow feels Polina's body losing strength as Willow pushes her towards the door. She throws Polina's coat over her shoulders and forces her to put her boots on. Mrs. Currie opens her car window slowly when the two women approach. Her face is white with fear when she sees Willow's bloody hand.

"Get off my property. And if I ever see you near my house again, I will have you arrested. Do you hear me, Mrs. Currie?" Willow's voice is calm, but there's no doubt she means what she is saying. Fire and fury blaze in Willow Alexander's eyes.

Mrs. Currie is silent.

Just then, Graham's car drives into the yard. Willow has never seen him so angry as he approaches his mother's car.

"I've called Polina's parents in New York," he says to his mother, trying to control his anger. "They've booked her a ticket. Her father will have a worker from the hospital pick her up at the airport. You will be responsible for taking her to the airport, since you encouraged her to come here." His voice makes it clear this is an order, not a request. "She's yours to deal with now, Mother. You invited her here. You take her back!"

Mrs. Currie steps hesitantly out of the car. "I am so sorry, Graham. I didn't know she was so crazy. You said nothing. Nothing! All these years with all this misery on your back. You're just like your father. You say nothing and go about like martyrs carrying a cross. He told me tonight what happened."

Polina slips her arms around Graham. He gently removes them and speaks to her softly.

"Polina, we are no longer man and wife. We haven't

been for a long time. We are divorced, you know that. Do you have your meds with you?"

Polina fumbles in her purse and takes out several bottles. Graham opens one and tips out two pills. He orders her to take them.

"No, Graham," Polina cries. "If I go back, my father will make me go back to that hospital! I want to live here with you. I will be good. I will be really good this time. I won't stab you ever again, like I did that time at the hospital."

"Polina, I'm sorry. I should never have married you. I should never have left here. This is where I belong. This is my home. You can't live here. Go back to my mother's house with her. She'll help you get back to New York." He places her in the front seat of his mother's car and commands his mother in a tone of finality, "Take her home!"

Polina shouts at him, "You don't love Willow. She looks like a chicken!"

Graham's mother is still crying, and screaming now as well. "I had no business bringing her here to look for you. She told me she was still married to you. I'm sorry, Willow. I had no idea what was going on. I had no idea how confused the woman is about everything."

Mrs. Currie backs down the driveway in tears. Polina slumps like a rag doll in the front seat.

After they drive away, Graham checks Willow's hand.

"It's just a scratch," she says, pulling her hand from Graham's grip.

"I'm sorry you had to witness this mess, Willow. She could have really hurt you," Graham says.

"I suspected something was wrong when she came to the door. She looked confused. I thought she might become violent," Willow responds as they walk into her house. "I wasn't wrong, but I was ready for it."

"Polina's been ill for years. I signed a contract for ten years at the clinic. It was never in her name. It wasn't a gift. Her parents put the clinic in my name, and I had to make the payments. She was diagnosed just after she graduated. She had her licence revoked years ago. I ran the clinic alone. I just threw myself into work and never said a word to anyone. I tried to get out of the clinic contract at first, but it would have cost me a fortune. So I counted the days until I could get back here. I finally sold the clinic, and I got my share of the sale. I left the other half in trust for her."

"I'm glad I finally know the truth. And I'm happy you finally put your mother in her place." Willow sighs.

"My father knew what was going on. He wanted to come and speak to you. But I begged him not to. I wanted to be man enough to tell you myself. I felt like such a loser."

"When were you going to tell me the real story, Graham?"

"When I thought you were ready to believe me, Willow. I feel so unburdened now. You know everything. Do you remember the day you and Marjorie and I were at the end of the wharf and the tide came up? I feel as free today as I did when we reached the sand." Graham takes a deep breath and exhales slowly. "I'll have to go back to my mother's house later. I want to be sure Polina is sedated for the night. Do you feel safe on your own here tonight? I can come back if you want."

"I'm safer than I've been in years," Willow says as she cups his face in her hands.

He holds her firmly in his arms. "Marry me, my Willow. I'll sleep in church the night before, so you'll know I'll be there in the morning."

Their laughter warms the kitchen.

Willow feels her life has finally been released from a place where time stood still, and when she looks back at where she's been, there are no longer any footprints to be seen. She realizes she doesn't have to return to a place where she really did not exist. The dead have finally moved on.

‡ ‡ ‡

LATER, WILLOW CAN hear a murder of crows cawing in the back field. Perhaps they are calling to one another to join the feast Willow has prepared for them.

"One crow sorrow, two crows joy . . ." she recites to herself in the empty kitchen, after Graham leaves.

She calls her friend Marjorie as Graham's car goes down the lane. "Guess what, my friend?"

"You're expecting, Willow."

"Hold on, Marjorie! I just cupped Graham's face in my hands."

"You're getting closer, Willow."

"I wanted to tell you who came to visit me today."

"It doesn't sound like a happy visit, Willow."

"No, indeed not, my friend. It was rather tragic, but it gave me the piece of the puzzle I've been wondering about for years. It was Graham's ex-wife. She's quite ill, a very sad, troubled soul. I'll fill you in later."

"What happens now, Willow? You know, now that the puzzle is complete?"

"I will never let Graham go again, Marjorie. He asked me to marry him. He even promised to sleep in church the night before, so I'll know he'll be there."

The girls share a long, hearty laugh.

"Good for him, Willow. I may stay with him to make sure he'll be there." She laughs again.

"There is more good news, Marjorie. I had an appointment with a specialist, and he believes with proper rest and tender loving care I could have a healthy wee one at my age. I'm over the moon. I believed time had run out for me to conceive."

"I'll be home soon, Willow. I'll be happy when this class is finished. I'm so pleased that I came back home to get this teaching degree in Halifax."

"Make it sooner, Marjorie. There are plans to be made, my friend."

CHAPTER THIRTY-THREE

A Slant in Stone

A WEEK LATER, FALL IS DROPPING SUBTLE HINTS around Glenmor as Willow rides up over the dusty hill and parks her car. She is going to meet with the young man from the construction company. In the cemetery, the burnished red sunset spills down like paint over the tall tombstones. A wind swirl rustles a few fallen leaves. Willow watches a black spider balance itself in the middle of a leaf. Her mother always believed that spiders were a sign of good luck. Willow smiles as she watches the leaf and its lone hiker parade out of sight.

The sound of music rolls down over the hill. The worker never labours in the graveyard without music. Willow hums along with the tune. The sign on the young man's truck comes into view as Willow walks towards the road. The worker steps out of his vehicle when he sees her approach.

"Are you a ghost or something?" asks the young man with a grin. "You're always hanging around here with the dead." He turns down his portable radio.

"My parents are buried beside the plots you're working on." Her voice is cool. "I told you that when we met before."

"Oh, yeah, I remember now. Something's different. You look younger or something."

"Or something," Willow replies. "I would like to have a tombstone repaired. It's tilted. I want it done before it falls over, as I mentioned to you on the phone."

"I had a look at it before you came. It'll cost a few bucks, for sure. The ground will have to be dug out around it, then firmed up. And it'll need a new cement foundation underneath, more than likely."

"I'm not worried about the cost. How about next week? Sometime soon."

"No problem. I'll hafta have a couple of guys with me to do the job right." He glances at Willow to make sure she isn't going to object.

"Might as well give his buddies a little work," Willow thinks. "Share the wealth."

"I should be finished with these here plots tomorrow. I have another job waiting in Baddeck, but it won't take too long. That new doctor that moved here was pretty anxious to get things done. Paid me half before I even started, when he met me here the other day. I was surprised to see him, because a woman had called in the order."

Graham? It is Graham who paid this man to prepare a burial plot next to hers? It's Graham who plans to lie three or four feet away from her for eternity? Has he actually measured the distance between them? Willow looks around, hoping the young man will not see her face, but he's already back in his truck, waving goodbye.

Her eyes rest on the towering maple tree that stands between the two family plots. When it's in full leaf, the tree will reach across their graves like a giant umbrella. She imagines what it will look like years from now. Birds will perch in the tree, singing sweetly. Mating. Young lovers might even stop by and wonder why Willow's and Graham's headstones are so close together. And they might even make up stories, just as she and Graham used to do about Mary Ann and John Duncan.

‡ ‡ ‡

WILLOW WALKS BACK to her car. She has a spring in her step. Her feet clang in the loose gravel as if she has tin cans on her shoes. She is laughing. She feels weightless.

Willow smiles to herself as she eases in behind the wheel of her car. She turns the car towards the Shore Road. A small ship drifts past the horizon, spreading an orange flame across the water. Willow has not walked along the shore since she carved the name Gabriel in the wet sand. She decides to go for a walk along the water. As she strolls along the shore, two young children walk along the loose waves of the sea towards her, their arms dangling at their sides. A few steps later, Willow stumbles over a piece of driftwood and falls to the ground. The young people run up to help her.

"Are you okay?" the boy asks. "I'll go get the doctor from the clinic. He lives there. My sister will stay with you. I can run faster than her."

"I remember you from the clinic," the girl says to Willow. "Your knee looks hurt real bad."

"I tripped over the log. It had a nail in it and now the nail is in my knee," Willow replies, breathing deeply to control the pain. "I'm so happy you children are here."

The sun is beginning to go down. What is left of the evening is hemmed in by fog. Willow buttons up her sweater and tucks her good knee close to her chin. She knows she shouldn't move. Graham will have to pull the nail from her knee.

The fog thins out and a lazy half moon waltzes in and out between the random clouds. Willow hears the opening and closing of a car door. Graham appears quickly at her side, placing something under her knee and strapping it down.

"You'll need stitches, Willow," Graham says. He then thanks the kids and tells them he will see them another time to reward them for their help. They run off towards their home. Graham helps Willow to his car.

At the clinic, Willow is his patient once again. She looks up at the circular light above the examining table. "How bad is my knee?"

"I'm going to give you a tetanus shot before I stitch it up. Would you like something for the pain?"

"No. I have to meet the young man from the graveyard at ten o'clock tomorrow. He is going to straighten Mary Ann up."

Graham laughs. "I'll take care of it for you, Willow. You'll be off your feet for a while."

Willow feels the prick of a needle in her arm—the tetanus shot—and another sharp pain from a sedative syringe. She watches the light drift away.

Afterwards, Graham carries the sleeping Willow up to his bedroom and lays her gently on his bed. He knows she will be asleep for hours. Graham goes back downstairs and tidies up his examining room, trying to keep busy. Willow, upstairs, in *his* bed? The thought is almost too much to process.

When Graham returns to check on her later, Willow is awake. While she slept, he sat on Kathleen's balcony, to clear his head. Willow picks up the scent of summer's end on his skin, a scent that freshens the air with a soft chill at the beginning of a new season. Willow offers Graham a seat next to her on the bed. He reaches over and checks the dressing on her wound.

"I thought you would sleep for hours," Graham says.

"I couldn't sleep. I wanted to ask you something."

"It's taken care of, Willow. They'll be working on Mary Ann's tombstone next week."

"That's good. But that wasn't the question."

She notices his shoulders droop. He looks wary of any more questions that she might want answered.

"Remember the little sparrow we buried on the school hill when we were kids? What do you think happened to that sparrow?"

"It lost its way. It wasn't a mature sparrow. Its wings weren't fully developed. It tried to fly, but it fell down." He looks at her for a moment. He realizes, maybe for the first time since his return, that Willow Alexander is no longer his enemy. Even injury and drugged sleep don't diminish the beauty he still sees in her face. "What made you think of the sparrow after all these years?"

Willow smiles. "You did, Graham. You brought that little sparrow back into my mind. It never left Glenmor. Maybe that's why I never left. Probably because I knew you would return one day."

"I hope you didn't stay around to bury this little sparrow when it returned," Graham said with a half grin.

"Looks like you've already taken care of that. I saw your gravesite, and it's very close to mine."

"It is, isn't it," Graham replies. "Close enough for you to fall for me again and we can finally get married."

Willow locks his gaze with her own. The silence between them lingers.

"Graham, do you think it is possible for me to carry a baby full term? I went to see a specialist. He said it was possible with lots of care." She smiles as she waits for his answer.

A smile coasts across his face. "Yes, but only if you stay away from nails. I see no reason why not, as long as you are healthy and remain so, with lots of rest and tender loving care. And the wedding will have to be sooner than later, my dear."

"I'm ready now, Graham. I can't put time on hold."

"You'll have to wait a few weeks, Willow, and let your knee heal."

Willow sees, on the bedside table, the photo of herself in her wedding gown. She reaches for it. "Nobody knew the secret that grew behind those fresh wildflowers," she says. "A gift wrapped as tight as skin, out of sight. The baby can't be remembered because he left no memories. But he did have a name, Graham. A name I've never revealed to anyone."

Graham turns to face the window. She can feel his body trembling.

Willow reaches over and takes his hand. "Look at me, Graham."

He turns slowly to face her.

"His name is Gabriel."

Epilogue

A FEW MONTHS AFTER GRAHAM CURRIE RETUR-
ned to Glenmor and set up a thriving practice, he
shed a noticeable amount of weight. He cares for
his patients in dark dress pants with the sleeves of his white
shirt rolled up, and they bring him meat pies and fish cakes
and parcels of sweets because they believe he has lost too
much weight.

The cremated bodies of Kathleen and James Millhouse
were returned out west. Their ashes now lie side by side, in a
cedar box. After their funeral, under a dusky purple sky and
a rumble of distant thunder, they were buried in a sudden
snowstorm. Willow likes to believe they got their last wish:
deep white silence.

Marjorie MacInnis turned the key in her newly built
house on the old family property. She used the money from
her late husband's insurance to build the home. She hung a

mop over the clothesline for old times' sake. Willow's gift to her was a framed copy of *The Ambassadors of the Fields*, and it hangs in her front entrance. Marjorie had fire extinguishers installed in every room of the house. Her parents returned to Glenmor to live with her the following spring. Marjorie is now the new grade one teacher at Glenmor School.

Shortly after returning to New York City, Dr. Polina Rebane died from an undisclosed cause in the psychiatric hospital. Her body was sent to Estonia for burial three days later. She was still wearing the wedding ring she had purchased for herself with the initials P and G engraved in silver.

Mrs. Currie slows her tongue to a crawl whenever she speaks with Willow. She is always polite and respectful towards Willow now. She never mentions Polina Rebane's name. It was Graham who told Willow of Polina's death. He had received a note from her parents. It included a cheque for the other half of the clinic. In her will, Polina had left everything she owned to her ex-husband, Graham Currie.

Speculation ran rampant when an old Model T was hauled into Glenmor on a rope one afternoon and parked on the Alexander property. Graham had bought it from an elderly patient who was happy to get rid of "the old piece of junk." The car was given a good going-over and painted a shiny red, and silver hubcaps were addeed. A new horn was installed along with a recycled engine. Its seats were upholstered in red leather. The parish hall was also given a fresh coat of paint. The church bells were realigned and polished. The organ was tuned and refinished to its original lustre. A new roof was added to the old white church. Dr. Graham and Willow covered all of these expenses. And to no one's surprise, the wedding banns of Willow Alexander and Graham Currie were announced in church one foggy Sunday morning.

Everyone for miles around was invited to the ceremony. Willow found her mother's wedding dress and veil in a trunk and aired them out. Marjorie was outfitted in a forties maid-of-honour gown in pale yellow. Dr. Graham and his best man, Colin, were decked out in top hats and tails. Crowds lined both sides of the road as Mr. Currie drove by after the ceremony in the Model T of his dreams. The happy couple waved from the back seat. Confetti covered the car like a soft snowfall.

After the reception and dance that evening, Willow and Graham drove back to the Alexander home under a harvest moon. He parked the Model T close to the front door. He carried his bride into the house and turned off the porch light, and slipped a DO NOT DISTURB sign on the door handle with a smile.

Ten months later, Willow strolls in the Journey's End Cemetery towards the open book-shaped headstone of her parents with her and Graham's baby daughter, Rhona

Alexandra Currie, cooing softly in her pram. She has chosen this special evening to introduce her new red-haired baby to her grandparents. Her daddy is out on a house call. As she walks back home, she remembers fondly Kathleen Millhouse's words about her relationship with her husband James:

"You know, Willow," she whispered, "he is my day and I am his night."

Acknowledgements

T HANKS TO ALL WHO UNWRINKLED THIS MANU-
script and let it flow. To Iris Tupholme for her acceptance of my words, to Karmen Wells and Janice
Zawerbny, for stroking my beloved Cape Breton with a soft
pen. And to Leo MacDonald, whom I happened to meet,
word for word, and who got everything going for me at
HarperCollins. To Pat O'Neil and her dedicated hours of
redirection. To my beautiful law student and granddaughter Clare Flynn, and my handsome grandsons Avery Veber,
Aidan and Caelan MacNeil, may your goals be complete in
every chapter of your lives. To Father George MacInnis, a
gifted musician and friend, I wish to dedicate to his dear
mother, the late Christie MacInnis, of Big Pond, Cape
Breton, the fictional Christie's Mountain that appears in
my novel.